T0158935

Ted Wall,
A Story of Sin

MARK PEEBLES

authorHOUSE®

AuthorHouse™
1663 Liberty Drive
Bloomington, IN 47403
www.authorhouse.com
Phone: 1 (800) 839-8640

© 2017 Mark Peebles. All rights reserved.

No part of this book may be reproduced, stored in a retrieval system, or transmitted by any means without the written permission of the author.

Published by AuthorHouse 08/22/2017

ISBN: 978-1-5462-0563-0 (sc)
ISBN: 978-1-5462-0562-3 (hc)
ISBN: 978-1-5462-0561-6 (e)

Library of Congress Control Number: 2017913068

Print information available on the last page.

Any people depicted in stock imagery provided by Thinkstock are models, and such images are being used for illustrative purposes only.
Certain stock imagery © Thinkstock.

This book is printed on acid-free paper.

Because of the dynamic nature of the Internet, any web addresses or links contained in this book may have changed since publication and may no longer be valid. The views expressed in this work are solely those of the author and do not necessarily reflect the views of the publisher, and the publisher hereby disclaims any responsibility for them.

DEDICATION

This book is dedicated to everyone. Those who exist, those who have existed and those yet to exist. Those who choose and forge their own path, with the ability to make life as they seem fit. The age-old question of what happens when we die might stay a mystery forever, but what isn't a mystery is the life that stands before us everyday we wake up and present ourselves to the world. This book is dedicated to the lovers, the free thinkers and the ones who will continue to promote the well being and love for all mankind for generations to come.

PROLOGUE

It was an interesting feeling, like being asleep but being suspended high above the ground. I could see a faint light above me and a faint light below me, and I had the feeling I was slowly moving down. I couldn't for the life of me remember how I got in this predicament but I was here, and with no sound and nothing around me my mind had plenty to contemplate.

What was the last thing I remember? Where was I last? Why am I here? I was lost.

The light below me started to grow, and I was slowly falling towards it. I started to hear things and see things, but I could not yet take in anything. Like the feeling of an astronaut coming back to earth, my body sensed the pull of gravity for the first time in what seemed like days. Patterns started to form, yet without any rhyme or reason. When I descended into the atmosphere of this new place, my brain started functioning at a level for me to come to realization. When the soles of my feet hit the ground my mind went on a frantic tangent. There was someone approaching me. I wanted to run, scream and wake up from this nightmare, but as the figure grew closer I became calmer, because it looked like it was just a normal guy. For the first time in a long time, I heard words spoken. "Welcome, my name is Chad, nice to meet you."

1

"I have questions," I explained, and he nodded at me and motioned a clipboard in his hand for me to follow him. "Once you pass clearance we will de-brief you," he said, his smug look glimmering under his bleached blonde hair. He walked me through walkways and hallways, occasionally beeping an access card on the wall before a door, and even speaking for voice recognition for another. The final door we entered was double enforced steel, and as we entered I saw others for the first time.

"I'll wait for you, you might want to grab a number," he said, as he was walking away towards what looked like coffee and cookies. *Come on Chad grab me some*, I thought to myself as I approached the counter.

I won't lie to you; the clearance looked and felt a lot like the Department of Motor Vehicles, but oddly better. Better because even though I knew I would have to wait, I didn't feel like I was in a rush to get anywhere else. I grabbed a form and a number and sat down. The form started normal but it got very personal, very quick. Name, date of birth, social security number, all the normal things, even though I was wondering why they even need this information, I'm sure if I am here they already have all the answers they needed. The questions quickly changed, as I had to answer surprising things.

"Hey Chad, can you come over here?" As I said that, he took the last bite of his cookie and last sip of coffee and sauntered over...*typical.*

"What's going on?" he said in a very...Chad way.

"This form is asking me extremely personal things, and I am wondering why this information is necessary, like for example, question forty-one asks, please provide size (if male), and if are you satisfied with it?"

Chad grinned and just simply replied, "the quicker you fill it out the quicker we can move on." Answer after answer I wrote down a synopsis of my whole life on a piece of paper, and walked back over and submitted it. The woman who took the paper looked at it, put it through what looked like a copy machine and quickly gave it back to me covered in red smears.

"What's wrong?" I proclaimed, ready to move on.

"The red is where you lied, we need the truth." She quickly looked down and continued to read her paper in front of her, and my paper beckoned.

Okay, let us try this again. I didn't want to write the truth, because honestly, I have slept with my best friend's girlfriend. I have taken a family member for granted, and yes, maybe an inch more would be nice. When I walked back over to her she was surprised with my haste. She once again scanned the paper, and with minimal red, she cleared me. Chad waved his hand, and I was on my way. *Thanks Glenda*, I thought to myself, as the smirking woman behind the counter now knew more than anyone I had known. I could have sworn I saw her laugh, but the room change blocked my view. *Whatever.*

"I'm assuming you want to know the full parameter of what's going on," Chad said as we walked into an overly open room.

"I feel like I am ready, but at some point, you have to tell me why I just wrote down on a piece of paper how I hung a toilet paper roll."

"All part of the process, let's keep going." Chad was talking and walking with a purpose. The open room we were walking through narrowed, and soon I saw other rooms. The décor became more gothic, and soon there were rooms every ten feet. "Room forty-seven, this is yours, make yourself comfortable and we will be back to pick you up later." Chad said this, but I couldn't help wondering who 'we' was. He walked away tapping his clipboard, and I entered my room.

It wasn't that bad, the carpet yearned for my bare feet. The bed hung onto me as I laid on it, and the shower must have been the size of my dorm room. I still felt completely lost into what happened and why I was here, but so far, I felt like I was in control, nothing felt overwhelming. It didn't take very long before I heard a knock at my door, and without a peephole I just had to open it. I realized in that moment my sandals, shorts and shirt were all feeling a bit worn, and I hoped my appearance wasn't under scrutiny. When I opened the door, my stomach twisted and my heart lifted off, I wasn't ready.

"Hello there, may I come in?" The blonde woman softly said, as she walked in and sat on my bed.

"You're Marilyn Monroe." The words fell out of my mouth on the floor, barely making sense.

She giggled and threw her hair back and nodded. "That is who I am, but they sent me to find out who you are." Her eyes as she talked sliced through me.

"What would you like to know Marilyn, it is a pleasure by the way to meet you." I stuttered and fell over myself.

"Stop! This is about you." She again threw her hair and arms back; she looked like she was floating.

"Well, where should I start, my name is Theodore Wall, but I go by Ted, and I just arrived here today." As I spoke she has her head now in her hands staring at me, hinting to go on. "I am, well was, thirty-seven years old and I am about as simple as a man can and could be. I had a dog, a mortgage, and an ex-wife." My brain started to fire, for some reason seeing Marilyn things started coming back to me.

"What happened?" when she asked, my gut knew it was coming. I didn't know how to answer though, because that question was loaded.

"I don't know what happened, I wish I did," I returned with an answer as loaded as her question. A silence fell over the room and she leaned her head back and stared at the ceiling and I could have sworn I saw a tear come out of her eye.

"I always get overly emotional, even with people I have just met" she rolled over on her stomach and covered her face with her hands.

"You always seemed like such a loving person, you do have a lot of coverage still!" As I said that she lit up but then quickly deflated again.

"My only fault was I loved too much, and deep down I feel like that is how I ended up here." She was facing away from me; I was starting to feel emotional now.

"Marilyn, I need answers. I need to know why I am here, and what I am supposed to do now." She rolled back over with misty eyes, and slowly got up.

"You will learn soon that the decisions you have made in the past will directly affect your immediate future, and my only advice is to enjoy the ride," as she proclaimed that haunting statement, she got up and motioned me for the door. "Come on, let me show you around before the de-brief."

My mind was having a tough time contemplating that I was locked arms with Marilyn Monroe walking around a gothic facility that was, even though it still seemed far-fetched, some sort of dreamlike purgatory. She pointed things out quickly and walked with a bright step, and after a while I kind of started feeling reminiscent like I was a new kid in school and this was my orientation. A work out room, a library, even a nap room resembling what I saw in movies about tech companies in Silicon Valley.

"Marilyn, all of this doesn't seem bad at all, but there has to be some sort of catch isn't there?" She looked at me, giggled, and nodded. Even though I was completely smitten by her, she had a haunting quality about her. *There was a catch, something isn't right.* I continued my tour and finally was left alone for a moment as Marilyn ran through the Cafeteria area we were in towards a group of guys who were ecstatic to see her. She motioned me to come over but I didn't budge, I felt uncomfortable knowing that I didn't know the full picture, and my hesitance brought a worried look from her.

"Ted, nice to see you out and about. It looks like Marilyn has shown you around a little." Chad's voice was whiny, but nonetheless it was nice to hear his voice, my mind needed ease.

"Chad, I need to know, what is the end game here? Am I here forever? I have never been good at making friends, and I don't like to admit I get jealous quickly too."

I shot a quick glance over to the crowd Marilyn had, all male and all interested in what she had going on.

Chad continued, "Tonight I am coming to your room and taking you to de-briefing. Try to relax and get a bite to eat before then, maybe meet some people." He tapped his clipboard and walked away.

I walked over to where the food was, and felt a pair of hands on my shoulders.

"Are you okay? I have some people for you to meet!" Marilyn drew me in again after five minutes of being away, though it felt like a lifetime.

I grabbed a piece of pizza and a coke and joined her group. I sat down at the table, and introduced myself.

"Hello everyone, my name is Ted Wall. Nice to meet you."

As I scanned the audience I knew no one sitting around me. I got waves and smiles thrown back at me, and my mind processed everyone.

"Hello Ted and welcome. You seem calm, that's nice. I wish everyone here had your demeanor." "My name is Tyler, and these are my friends Max and Fred." As he mentioned them they waved hello and continued to eat.

"How'd it happen?" Tyler continued.

He looked at me with intent but before I could answer Marilyn interjected, "He just got here, and he hasn't even been de-briefed yet." As she said that all three guys gave me a discerning look, but kept a calm demeanor.

"Well Ted, I wish you luck, I really do, and just remember, the decisions you have made in the past will directly affect your immediate future." That was the second time I had heard those words in a matter of a couple hours, and I began to feel sick. Max and Fred tried to approach me with conversation, but I got up and just blankly walked away. I put out my hand to tell Marilyn not to follow, and made it back to room forty-seven.

2

"*It's time.*" Hearing Chad through the door woke me up; I had slept so deeply I felt like I was being born again. I opened the door and Chad guided me out of the room and down the hall. At that moment, I didn't feel like talking, but my mind wandered. I didn't have a clue how long I had been down here. Chad opened a door, and welcomed me inside, and I was greeted by a long wooden table with about twenty or so seats, and he asked me to sit. I noticed Chad had freshened up a little bit, blazer and jeans donned his small Chad like frame.

The door on the opposite side of where we entered swung open, and in walked a man with an opposing figure, must have been a six-foot seven-inch frame to my guess, and about as bald as a man can be.

"Thank you, Chad, that will be all." As the mystery man spoke Chad got up, patted me on the shoulder, and walked out. The mystery man opened a folder, and in lied my documents where I had to tell the truth, the whole truth, and nothing but. He cleared and throat and looked up at me, and gazed into my soul.

"Hello Ted. I hope you want answers, because that's all I have for you." His words hung in the air, and I nodded, unable to speak. "I have good news and bad news for you." "First, you are not in hell. Well, not technically." As he said that I perked up and darted a glance at him, but I couldn't interject before he kept going. "This is an area of space between heaven and hell that you have come to and you need to find full resolution." He spoke with such purpose.

"So, am I dead?" my words floated towards him, and he seemed to smile, as he knew the question was coming.

"Yes, Ted you are. Well, kind of, it's complicated," as he finished speaking I felt every cell in my body tense.

"So, what am I doing here?" I asked sharply. "To decide what the next step is, which is the bad news, a lot of the work is yet to be done." he spoke so calmly, as my emotions spiked. "What more could you need of me, what else can I do, what is going to happen next?" I fired questions at him like a machine gun. "Slow down Mr. Wall, let's take a walk."

"Right now, there are four hundred and seven people here, awaiting resolution. Some of the people have been down here for what is on Earth years' worth of time, and some people like you have been down here for just mere hours." As he continued it answered my sense of time, I was relatively fresh. "You are a special case though Ted, and I'm afraid that the next words out of my mouth might upset you, but you need to stay calm." He spoke with such calm demeanor, but as we walked the halls past random people doing random things, my mind went blank.

"What could you possibly tell me that is worse than me being dead and awaiting resolution to the next step of this pit?"

He took in my concern, and spit the most disturbing six words back at me… "Your wife is down here too."

Like the first hill on a roller coaster, my stomach seized to the point of pain. I had questions, I had thoughts, but my mind was in shock.

"Mary Ann can't be down here, what could have possibly happened?" He waved his hand to lead me into an office that was dark and cool, and sat me down.

"She was received by Keith right around four minutes after your arrival, and if you had turned around once and looked back, I have no doubt you may have even seen her." As he spoke he poured what looked like scotch, took a swig and swallowed hard.

"Can I see her? Can I talk to her? What do I do?" He got pummeled with my questions.

"Look, Ted, there will be interaction down here but it against protocol to have family or spouses interact before resolution is complete." Another pour, another swig.

"Then tell me, what is resolution?" He perked up. That was the question he was looking for.

"Ted, you are going to be put on trial, and the reason why we have to act quickly with you is because we cannot do anything with Mary Ann until we resolve you." Yet another pour, another quick swig.

"By the way you are drinking I feel like I may be fighting an uphill battle" I spoke, like an angry mother at him at a holiday dinner table.

"Ted, this trial is not like your trial you may be used to, this is a trial of your sins, and will determine your fate." He put the drink away, and sat in his chair facing away from me. "This will be the hardest thing you have to face and witness, and it will be out of your control. You will be a spectator, and you will see the ultimate hand of fate decide, and it will be focused completely on you." He didn't move, but he seemed to steady himself.

"What does this all mean?" I didn't have much to say, this was all hitting me too quickly.

"Ted, heaven and hell are going to fight for you, and they are going to bring up all the beauty of your life, and all the darkness. They have elite teams designed to examine your life in seven different ways, ultimately being able to decide at the end whom receives you." He swung back around and looked at me.

"I don't know what to say, I don't think this could get any worse" I was lacking words to express how I truly felt.

"It does get worse though Ted. Your wife will attend the trial."

As numbness swept over my body I got up and poured myself a drink to no protest from my mystery keeper of bad news.

"What is your name anyways? All this talking and I don't even know your name." I looked at him as I poured alcohol down my throat.

"My name is Ted too," he spoke calmly, hinting that he did not need a reply. "I wish you luck." In your room tonight you will get the full details on how this will all go down, and all I can do now is wish you luck, and to remember to stay strong." As he finished speaking, the door opened and Chad was waiting.

Chad didn't speak as we walked down the hallway back towards the common area, and the whole time we walked I scanned for a sight of my wife. Chad wasn't very lively as he was when I first met him, and as we approached my room, he shot me a conservative glance, nodded, and guided me in.

I was once again alone, and the time between the first time I entered this room and the second time came with such heavy consequence. With the thought of a trial and my wife, so much information needed digestion with such little time to process it because at that moment I heard a knock on my door. No words were exchanged between the messenger and I as I was presented with a blank envelope that was not sealed. I walked over to the bed, sat back Indian style and opened it. Inside the envelope was my fate, and for the first time since I died, I felt alive again.

The letter had bold black writing, and stated all the needed facts I was looking for, but who composed it was the most surprising.

Dear Ted,

I hope this letter finds you well. The past couple hours must have been grueling for you, as I know they are for a lot of people in your predicament. You should know though, I see a lot of potential in you, and I am hoping the resolution that awaits you is in your favor. Call me an optimist but I enjoy the brighter side over the darker side, and I have fought for that idea for a long time. Your fate will be known within seven days' time, and within this seven-day period you will be on trial for each of the seven deadly sins. In this trial, you will have a team from heaven defending you and a team from hell prosecuting you, and unfortunately you will be a spectator. As you may have heard before the decisions you have made in the past will directly affect your immediate future. That statement rings true as your life will be put in the spotlight, and your fate will be decided. Each night if the ruling favors heaven, you will be able to spend the night in heaven. Conversely, each night that the ruling favors hell, you will be in hell. Stay strong, and keep your wits about you. Good luck, and I hope to meet you soon.

Sincerely yours, as I may go by many names, simply put, God.

I sat back and tried to digest what I had just read. Yet even a letter from 'God' himself couldn't take the fact that Mary Ann was down here, and that I needed to reach her before this trial went down. I laid the letter down on my nightstand and walked into the bathroom. I splashed water on my face with force and slapped my face a couple times, albeit not hard, just enough to remind myself I was still a conscious being. Although I could feel the slap, deep down I wish it woke me up from what was now feeling like the most vivid dream I had ever experienced. I got my wits about me and swiftly left my room.

3

If I was going to find her I would probably have to find other areas I had not yet explored before. *Follow the white rabbit...*my mind was all over the place. I had never digested this much information in one day. The main lobby was dim, it kind of felt like since the first time I was there things had calmed a bit, a with the candles in the cubbies lit it gave a gothic tranquil essence. The first thought that crossed my mind was to ask someone if they had seen her, but Ted's words stuck in my head, I couldn't see her before tomorrow. As I walked into an undiscovered hallway I could hear music, laughter and talking. I followed the sound and I uncovered what felt like a traditional mid-western dive bar right off this main hall.

It was amazing as everyone I passed had such a calm demeanor to them, talking away, laughing away. My mind raced again as tunnel vision set in a bit. What are they talking about? Why are they laughing and what are they laughing at? Are all these people awaiting trial? I walked up to the bar area and sat down, keeping my head on a swivel to see if I could spot her.

"What would you like my friend?" spoken with such ease, a smiling bartender stared at me.

"Yeah hello, I don't know. How about a beer?" I scanned the back bar and everything was blank, confusion set in.

"Which beer would you like? "I have everything," again with the smile and the stare.

"Well, how bout Pliny the Elder, from Russian River Brewery in Sonoma California." I wanted to challenge him, and smirked as I did.

He walked back, grabbed a glass, and took the blank draft handle and poured. I recognized the golden hue the second it cascaded out.

"Nice choice sir. Let me know if you would like anything else" he walked away, and I could swear his smile got larger. I took a sip, and the aromatic hop spice hit my palate. If this was a perk of being dead, I could get used to it.

I slid away from the bar and scanned again, with the area I was in about half full I had garnered up the liquid courage to speak with someone. I sat down across from an older gentleman, and he wasted no time conversing with me.

"Yes sir, how are you? Hello, hello…" he spoke with a reckless abandon. "I hope you don't mind, since they allow it all I enjoy it all, and I just roll with the punches." He put emphasis on 'roll' as he pulled out a bag of marijuana and some rolling papers, and effortlessly was lifting off in moments. He passed the joint over to me, and before I even inhaled for the first time he was rolling another. When I motioned the joint back, he chuckled and calmly gestured for me to keep it.

"So, what is your name son?" he seemed calm as he flew.

"Ted, I just got here. I have just received a bunch of information all day, and they are putting me on trial tomorrow for my full resolution." as that sentence came out of my mouth I realized I was now high, and it felt nice.

"Well, so quick, I am impressed. They have been holding me here for eleven years, every time I ask they say they are still compiling information on me." He rolled another joint, and lit it from the candle in the middle of the table.

"Compiling information? It seemed like they had mine done before I even got here." I talked, but my mouth started to dry, I took a swig of beer and refreshed.

"Son, when you come down after sixty-seven years it may take longer to compile information, especially when you have seen and heard what I have. I imagine my trial being full of laughter, tears, and a bout of motion sickness, especially if they are watching it from my point of view." When he said that I chuckled a bit, until I realized that my trial was tomorrow, and that it would be from my point of view.

"I guess there are advantages to coming down here young then, I was only thirty-seven, but I never thought I hadn't lived a full life. I was always talking about all that I had accomplished in my time, but now that it is over, I wish I had done more." After this sentence, I felt sad for the first time. I sat back, took a long drag and another swig, and examined my conversation partner. "You haven't told me your name," I calmly said, hinting at the fact that I was enjoying talking with him.

"I apologize, my mind has always moved faster than my words. Hunter Stockton Thompson. It is truly a pleasure to speak with you."

As my mind realized that I had been speaking to the godfather of gonzo himself, I felt four long fingernails on my back.

"Sweetheart, I have to get you back to your room. You have such a long day ahead of you tomorrow." As I looked up I saw Marilyn's eyes gleaming back at me. She had a look to make a man leave their mind for a moment, and float in pure bliss.

"Marilyn, have you met Hunter?" Hunter did a half bow, and smiled.

"Of course, one of my dear friends here. He is always such a joy to talk to, but my mind can't keep up with him."

Hunter laughed and rolled yet another, and motioned for us to go. "Good luck Ted, stay strong." "Life is what you made of it...." as he said that, I realized his use of tense. I shook his hand, smiled at him and walked away.

Maybe it was the flight I was on, or the liquid I had devoured, but I did feel calm.

"Marilyn, my wife is down here. I have a trial tomorrow, I am nervous about all of this." I felt like a lost child looking for truth in life.

"Sweetheart I know all of this, and I am here to help in any way I can." As she spoke we sat on a padded bench, I instantly became comfortable. "If you must know, it isn't all that bad. Hell can be a bitch, but heaven is everything it is cracked up to be."

I glanced at her with a need for understanding. "Marilyn, you have been to both places?" She shied away, but met my eyes again.

"Yes, they put me on trial fifty-three years ago, and I almost made it through, but I couldn't bear anymore with so many loved ones being there. I lived my life the way I wanted to, and I felt like I was able to make an impact. Yet when I was sitting there I was reminded of all the negative impact I had. I couldn't listen to them speak anymore, I requested a recess, and they granted me with one that has lasted decades. I became accustomed to this lifestyle, and I got used to it." She welled up, and I truly didn't know how to respond.

"Are you able to go back?" So much information being digested again, but this was personal, it felt real.

"Anytime I would like." Her answer surprised me. As I contemplated a reply, I saw something in the distance that had the look I had been searching for.

It is she; I was speed walking through the lobby resisting Marilyn's pleas to stop. I started to full out sprint towards the figure I saw, and my mind was recognizing more and more as I approached her. I reached out my hand towards her dirty blonde hair and her elegant frame, but as I turned her around the figure became larger, and was not the love I was searching for. It was Ted, and as he grew from a crouch to his full frame he looks genuinely disappointed in me.

"I think you should call it a night Ted," he spoke with discernment and a smell of dark liquor hit me like a wall. Marilyn put her arms around me and pulled me away, my mind was still in disbelief, and it was she.

"Honey, you have to settle down. The reason why you can't see her is beyond your power, and you have to let it go for now," she spoke with concern, but care.

"It was Mary Ann, I swear on my life." I was still confused. As he turned around his frame became smaller and gentler, and from a distance I could have sworn it transformed again. In this moment, I realized even though I knew where I was, I was lost.

The next few moments were a blur, as I tried to comprehend the whole situation. I walked slowly, and Marilyn accompanied me all the way back to my room.

"Will you come in?" I spoke softly. Marilyn nodded, and guided me in. She sat me down on the couch across the room and walked over to a record player. She scanned the stand by it and pulled out her selection and positioned the needle. The moment it came on I recognized it automatically from the first note.

"I like to listen to music of the living. It helps me feel alive," she said so elegantly as the first verse of The Cave rambled on.

"I saw Mumford and Sons, they were amazing. I would even go as far to say that it was one of the best moments of my life. My wife was a huge fan, and she got us tickets in the third row. We were so immersed in the music it felt like I was floating." As I continued to speak, Marilyn smiled, but shot a glance of wonder and yearning.

"Tell me about your wife." Marilyn pulled her knees in towards her chest and reeled me in.

"She was, and still is my whole life. From the moment I first saw her to the moment I last saw her she always controlled my heart like no one else ever could. She was simple, yet complex. She was gentle, yet strong. She was loving, yet worrisome. My greatest regret is not saying goodbye, and that's why this is so hard. Death isn't made to be perfect, and I don't think anyone dies the perfect way, but if I could have controlled it, I would have kissed her just one more time."

Marilyn had tears in her eyes and they began to stream down her face. I quickly apologized for my rant, but she gave me a look of content.

"I love love. I always have," she smiled and gave a short laugh.

"I know you did. You left behind a legacy of love that hasn't been matched since you left."

She stared at me, and seemed to smile with an understanding of my comment. She slid over to me, and rested her head on my shoulder.

"Ted, I hope everything goes well for you, I really do." I took those words and stored them away as the best I had heard all day. I closed my eyes and took in the music.

As the next song came on, Marilyn perked up and grabbed my hand.

"Waltz with me!" She was now leading me around the room.

"I don't know how." I was embarrassed, but didn't care. As she glided around the room, I became transfixed. Our eyes met, and our bodies became one. She guided the waltz as Marcus Mumford continued his serenade. I eventually made my way back to the couch, and watched as Marilyn continued to dance. My eyes got heavy, and everything faded away.

4

My awakening felt truly like I was being born again, and even though I still felt lost, I had no panic or worry left in me. I looked around and did not see Marilyn anywhere, and the record had run its course. I walked over to the bathroom and took my time grooming and cleaning myself up. I proceeded to let the water in the shower run, focusing its energy on my shoulders, suspended in physical bliss. The clothing left for me to get dressed into was a black tuxedo, reminding me of the one I wore for prom. Memories flooded into my head just as the telephone began to ring. I picked up the phone to a familiar voice, albeit not the one I was looking for.

"Good morning, we leave in one hour. Grab some food in the lobby and we will be leaving," Chad spoke with such energy so early.

"Thank you," I shot at him as I dropped the phone and walked back into the bathroom.

I had never liked my hair fully groomed. The 'bed-head' look was what I aspired to everyday, but today was different. I parted my hair to the side and applied product to make sure it stayed for as long as it needed to. I applied a bit of a fragrance and stared in the mirror. *I must look good for her.* The thought overcame me and I felt worried, but took a deep breath and left my room.

The air in the hallway was fresh, and I felt a draft sweeping through. As I entered the lobby it was bright and full of life. I wasn't hungry, but I filled a plate anyways and went over and sat by myself. I poked and prodded at the food and let my mind wander, but it was just as I was fully recognizing my current situation that I saw her. My mouth went instantly dry and my heart slammed in my chest. *I didn't know I was going to see her here, and so soon.* She walked down the stairs in a long red dress, and her eyes darted across the room at me. The whole lobby stilled and became transfixed as her elegant frame floated across the floor. As she approached me I perked up and quickly tried to find the words to greet her with.

"Good morning Ted." As she spoke it was like I forgot what her voice sounded like.

"Good morning Marilyn." She put out her hand and I rose from the table, and she walked me across the lobby as all eyes stayed transfixed on her. As we walked I didn't speak, I just rode the energy she emitted and stayed calm. The draft I felt earlier was hitting me again, and I realized we were walking outside. I had not been outside since I first got here, and it was nothing as I remembered. Roses were in full bloom as we walked, and fountains rained water in beautiful ways. The smell of fresh apples was in the air, almost like an orchard was right around the corner. We continued to walk and my eyes again became smitten with Marilyn standing in front of me. We approached what looked like a train station, yet it was completely void of life and trains.

As we entered my thoughts were confirmed; it was a train station. All the benches were a deep brown colored wood that had the look and feel of Victorian elegance but were as smooth as silk. We both sat and I broke the silence.

"When do we leave?"

She looked and smiled.

"Soon dear, soon." As I looked around I spotted a clock and regained a sense of time once again. *Eight Thirty, a.m.* As I tried to combat the time a train approached, and we rose and walked over towards it. The insignia that was on top of the train car read 'TRS.' *What did that mean?* We stepped aboard and sat down, again the only two there.

Where is my wife? Where is everyone else? Who is everyone else? The rabbit hole was once again opening as the train began to move. Outside the scenery changed quickly, forest to beach, beach to desert, desert to mountain. I had no idea what to think, but once again heard Marilyn speak.

"Brings back memories and makes me feel anxious," she reminded herself of her own trial. I was at a loss.

"Why can't you just get through it? I am sure with the overall legacy you left heaven would be yours, no doubt," I smiled at her, she smiled back.

"Ted, you are way too optimistic for me, have you always been like this?" She smiled at me again and I replied.

"I had to be, growing up in small town Ohio there was always something wrong. Weather was the main one, then came money, and ultimately things fell apart without optimism." As I spoke, Marilyn again welled up, seeming to care beyond her control. "Also, when it comes to money, or weather or just everyday life, without love and your heart in the right place, life can truly seem heavy."

Marilyn put her head in her hands, and began to cry.

"I'm sorry, I didn't mean to upset you. I was just rambling." I put my arm around her and tried to apologize with my body language as well.

"Ted, they don't even let people who commit suicide go on trial, and when you said things fall apart, I couldn't help but think of all the people I never got to meet." Her eyes looked outside with a longing, and my heart grew heavy with the knowledge of some great people I knew that took their life. My mind became still, as the train rushed on.

After what seemed like forever, the train started to slow. My heart again started to race, and we were stopping at what reminded me of a corporate center in the middle of a big city. *This is not what I was expecting.* As we pulled up, the building adjacent to the train was all glass, and imposed itself with radiant sun beaming off in all directions. Marilyn shot up and beckoned me to follow, and off we were.

The doors of the building opened with ease, and hanging overhead was a marquee that simply read, "Ted Wall." As we walked in several levels were present to the eye, and random people were walking around. One sole woman sat at the desk in front of us, and she waved us over.

"Ted Wall, day one today," Marilyn spoke for me, and my mind was blank.

"Ah yes, follow me, I will show you the way." The woman speaking was professional; yet spoke with a calmness that haunted me. We started to walk off to the right of her desk down a walkway. The way we walked there were no rooms, there were no walkways, just one long narrow path. After what seemed like three or four football fields I saw two doors coming up ahead, the receptionist stopped and pointed, and began to walk back the way we came. As Marilyn proceeded forward, my legs became completely immobile. It took her a while to realize she was walking alone, and she hurried back to me when she saw me behind. She took me into her arms, and for the first time in what seemed like forever I just sat and cried. I cried into her arms, and after what seemed like hours, I composed myself.

"You'll be fine, I know you will." Although my first instinct was that she spoke with empty hope, after getting to know her better those seven words had me walking again. The room we walked into was intimidating. There must have been a thousand seats, three levels, and it showed itself as a hybrid of a movie/opera theater. The outside of the building had such a modern, clean feel to it, yet the second I walked into the theater it composed itself as Renaissance brilliance, and I felt like I was attending a Shakespeare comedy. There were two seats lit up in the front row and we quickly made our way to them, and every other sat behind us slowly became too dark to see.

"Welcome," a voice rang from the rafters, and my heart started up again. "Be still, we will begin soon." The voice was calm, but was nowhere close. As I let the silence hold in the room, people began to fill the seats behind me. I cocked my head in both directions and had an alarming realization. *She is here, somewhere sitting behind me.* Marilyn kept her eyes forward, and smiled at me as my first bead of sweat came down my brow. She leaned over and wiped it away and just hummed. *I know that song;* I thought to myself…*I love Dave Matthews…* Just hearing the words in my head calmed me as I looked forward again.

The room behind me was full, but completely still. Suddenly in front of us a large red curtain opened and in front of us was a table on each side, and a large projector screen in the middle. My heart was getting a workout today, but meeting eyes with Marilyn made me calm, because as she and others had said before, *I am going to be okay.* The voice once again roared above us.

"Welcome to the resolution of the life of Ted Wall. Presiding over this trial will be the prosecution from hell, known simply as 'The Circle' and the defense from heaven known simply as 'The Hope.'"

My eyes were honed in on the tables that sat vacant. Then, with a click and a swing, the door on hell's side swung open, and 'The Circle' made their way in. Although my overall advice was that I was going to be okay, in this moment as these four men walked across the stage, I felt like all hope was lost.

5

I was never a big history buff in school, and honestly, I didn't see the reason in focusing on what was in the past over what was in the present and in the future, but as these four men walked out, my brain was conjuring up any recollection I had for them, and how they may be affecting my current predicament. Hell seems like a very unpleasant situation to be faced with, and these four were the quote unquote leaders, which were prosecuting with the end goal of recruiting more to their dystopian world.

Deep down I knew Adolf would be there; when you have a conversation about evil in the modern sense Hitler becomes synonymous. Guilty of killing people in camps, creating a new world order, and igniting a World War that would grace every history syllabus for generations to come. Earlier Marilyn had mentioned to me that people who had committed suicide never go on trial, but I wonder if when he died, Hell was just waiting with open arms. Needless to say, having him walk out first was intimidating. Right behind him was another figure I recognized from my dosing days in third period, a man known simply as Joseph Stalin.

It also seemed as Adolf and Joseph walked in unison, and with each step they took, I could almost hear faint cries of the millions that had perished under their respective reigns. Intimidation settled in with the inclusion of those two, but fear set in with the other two that walked slowly behind them.

"Who is that, behind Stalin?" I quietly looked at Marilyn, careful not to cause too much commotion.

"That's Vlad Dracula, or otherwise none as Vlad the Impaler. I could go into more detail, but honestly, just know; he doesn't say much, yet he is the most ruthless of the four. He is born and bred with pure evil running through his veins, and he takes pride at this whole recruiting process." Marilyn stopped speaking and eased back.

Thank you, Marilyn, for the good news. As my mind thought about the horrible acts she was speaking of, I couldn't help but be transfixed on the last man walking behind the other three. I couldn't see him well, but my heart began to race as I starting to get a clearer view. *That's Ted.* Like my wild chase for my wife had been, I felt as though my mind was playing tricks on me.

"Marilyn, I know that man; he was the one who told me about my fate, and he was the one who I met when I raced towards my wife! Who is he?" I got frustrated, and as I spoke louder all four men glanced at me, and I became still.

The mixture of confusion, anger and fright that had been created inside of me was toxic. I had trouble breathing, swallowing, and I starting to lose feeling in some parts of my body. I was slowly becoming paralyzed by my own fear. If it wasn't for the next four people I saw to my right enter the room, I may have just seized and become completely immobile, but I quickly recognized all of whom they called 'The Hope' and my mind started to ease. Although not physically intimidating by any means, these people had an aura about them that was so potent the whole room seemed to reign applause down, even though you could hear a pin drop.

As legacies go, Leonardo Da Vinci will probably challenge any resume you have to offer. From his historic presence as an inventor to his lasting works as an artist, I almost became star struck at seeing him in the flesh. Marilyn giggled softly to herself, and I turned back and gave her an inaudible sigh of relief. Walking behind Leo was Martin Luther King Jr. and just the sound of his footsteps demanded attention; he out of the eight was whom I knew the most about after all my readings about the civil rights movements. His emotion and stature was that of legend, and just watching him grace the stage will forever be something that excited me, no matter where my final location may be. As much violence that 'The Circle" had under their belt, no one better than Mahatma Gandhi himself to counteract so perfectly. Physically he took none of the stage, but in the same breath seemed to own it. He had a slight smile, and he was the only one to look at me and acknowledge me as he came in. As I processed his presence my eyes couldn't comprehend the figure walking behind him. The short blonde cut, the blue eyes and the gentle figure crept out of the darkness. The last seven people that had presented themselves melted away, as my own mother walked out last.

I couldn't grasp the idea of her being here, but if there was anyone who knew my life held only good intentions it would be my mother. My whole life was dictated through two sets of eyes; as my mother and I shared a birthday, and with that shared a good portion of our soul. Just the fact she was accepted into heaven was a relief, but to see her come to my defense just proved as another moment I can never fully repay her for. I became quite uncomfortable as Ted on the other side was completely zeroed in on her, and it made me want to get up and not only protect her, but also question why he was here and why he had such a smug grin across his face. As all eight of them sat, the lights went down, and a single spotlight shone ahead.

A small, frail woman walked out from behind the curtain. Her steps didn't make a sound as she seemed to float along out into the middle of our vantage point. The fact that I didn't recognize her made me feel a bit anxious, as the emotion of the previous eight still weighed heavy on me. She raised an envelope up, and slowly slid a piece of paper out of it. As she unfolded the paper I snuck a look back at Marilyn, and her expression warmed my body, she just smiled at me with a sense of hope I desperately needed.

"Today, we are to speak about Lust." She spoke with such a presence that her physical nature was nowhere close to matching. "Lust can come in many forms, whether it be a physical lust for flesh, a mental lust for knowledge, or an emotional lust for power or control, it acts as one of the deadliest of sins. The ability to see is a fundamental sense of being able to carry out everyday life, but Lust has the power to blind even the keenest of sight. Lust is where we begin this trial of Ted Wall, and The

Circle, you may begin," the last words rang in the theater, and no one spoke or stood until she was gone. Then, a projector screen slid down in front of us, and the trial began.

As the generic countdown on the film began to run, I quickly shuffled over to Marilyn.

"What happens now?" I became a bit frantic, as seconds ticked.

"You do nothing. Each side is able to present their most lustful moment of your life, serving as a good thing and a bad thing, and a decision will follow," before I could respond to what she shed light on, the past came to life. My heart seized, and my eyes took in my life, all over again.

6

"Ted baby, can you grab my phone please, I have to call that asshole back really quick." Amy had such a seductive voice when she spoke; even the most routine commands became sultry. I threw the phone back over towards her, and as she rolled over to grab it I could see the dark curves of her back throwing the reflection of the computer screen back at me. I turned back away from her for a moment, and double clicked my playlist just simply titled "The right stuff" and music filled the room. *Where are you at right now? Where have you been all weekend? I am going to come get you.*

I couldn't help but channeling the other side of her conversation more than her side as the voice on the other side of the phone became clearer.

"Like I told you, my job wants me traveling to accounts more to broaden our outreach program. What was supposed to take a day took two, just relax." She even lied with such a tone that made me melt, as I combated letting guilt creep in. "Okay, just please keep me in the loop and I will see you when you get back, I love you."

As those three final words rang through the phone, she hung up and threw herself back at me. She was just someone I had seen in passing at my local dive. Every night she came in with her girlfriends, became the life of the dismal low key Mid-western party, and left arms locked with all her friends. I probably had given her a total of about nine words before tonight. My mind wandered to earlier in the night.

"Coming here alone, I just might be able to buy you a drink." I glanced at her as I spoke; I had a calm confidence when I was heavily intoxicated.

"I also came alone, and until you spoke I was still wondering who the loneliest person in this bar was." Her brown eyes sliced through me, I was hooked.

"Lonely is just a matter of perspective. I am not lonely, my friends Jack and Johnnie have been hanging with me all night," as I spoke I raised my glass to her, pointing at the bar bottles.

"Oh, I see, well, don't mind if I join," she took my glass, and downed the whole thing. If I was sober, I might have felt a bit overprotective, but as my shields lowered with every drink I had, her overstepping was just enough for me to float over the edge.

Alcohol was flowing with ease, and the second she went outside to her car for a cigarette, her body language told me she had no intention of coming back in. I followed anxiously. We swapped drags and the second the cigarette hit the ground; we got in the car to leave. Between the passionate kissing during her driving and the constant physical touching, my mind cannot recollect how we got back to my house that night. I was living alone at the time in a run-down duplex, and the second we hit my driveway we were in the backseat. As clothes hit the floor of the car, I couldn't help but hear the faint rumbling of a phone that was consistent as our physical demands were met.

"So, does the fact he thinks you are away on business mean we can stay together for another twenty-four hours before you are back to your man, and we are back to being friends?" As those words came out of my mouth I came to the realization that Amy had a boyfriend, and I didn't care at all. She uncovered herself, then came over and straddled me, and as we kissed again the world melted away, and my mind became blank.

A couple of weeks later, I was on the fourth hole of my home golf course, I missed two straight calls from a number that wasn't saved in my phone. As I birdied the fifth, I grabbed my phone and listened intently. As the voicemail went on, I could feel every single cell in my body tense, and I quickly grabbed my ball off the sixth tee, and drove back the clubhouse. I called back immediately as I got in my car, and tried to rationalize the previously recorded forty-seven seconds Amy left me. As she spoke, the memory of our forty-eight-hour weekend flooded me with intense feelings, but that were all clouded with regret.

"He doesn't know, but if we are going to make a decision on this we have to soon, because I am already a month in." Her words didn't register, and my silence provoked her into raising her voice.

"Just come over in the next hour or so; my front door will be unlocked," she hung up, and I continued driving. As I made my way into her driveway, I started to tense up thinking of the conversation to come.

"Hi Amy." That's all I mustered as I lazily made my way in.

"Come up here, I am in the bathroom." Her voice ignited me again; it was intoxicating.

"I feel like if we are to make a decision about this, it has to be thought out," she said as she stared right through me. "I don't even mind keeping what we have; I honestly wouldn't even bat an eye about ending it with this lowlife, he is really just wasting my time." My mind raced as she spoke, I remained speechless.

"I wouldn't want it to become a burden on you." I didn't know if those were the right words, but those are the words that came out.

She sat and stared at me, and as she looked back at the mirror in front of her, she began to cry. I walked over to her and put my arm around her, and even though she had a lot of angst towards me, she returned the touch.

"I always imagined myself as being a great mother Ted." She spoke with such honesty it hypnotized me.

"Amy, I have no doubt in the future you will be someday."

The lights slowly came back on, and again I easily felt the most uncomfortable I have ever felt in my whole entire existence. The Circle sat and quietly leaned over and whispered to each other, as The Hope sat silent. I felt a hand on my shoulder. As I turned back Marilyn leaned in and put both her arms around me in consolation, trying to take on some of the discomfort I emitted.

Is my wife here? What is coming next? How am I going to make it through all of this?

My mind didn't even have a chance to fully digest the uncovered truth in the room before the screen started to roll down again. *Please revive me*, I whispered as I calmed myself. I put my hand on top of Marilyn's and took a deep breath as The Hope displayed their rebuttal.

"It's a shame Mary Ann is going with that asshole Steve, but I don't think Ashley is a bad backup to have." Mike always had an optimistic view, even when it came to high school homecoming dances and my junior year crush.

"I won't lie, Steve is quite the character, but they have been dating for a good year and it was a given they were going together." Even though my reply was simple, my thoughts on the matter remained complicated. "Mary Ann knows you like her, and she flirts with you all the time. The way Steve treats her has to be beyond frustrating. You can tell he just doesn't care at all about her feelings!" As he spoke I got frustrated with my predicament, and started to feel as though having nothing to lose was the best-case scenario.

"Hey, I am going to take Ashley to go grab a drink; we will be back." As the girls walked away my eyes became transfixed on Mary Ann, and how she danced with Steve like they were on fire. When he walked away to go meet up with some of his friends, I swooped in.

"May I have this dance?" I grabbed her hand and hip, and pulled her close.

"Well hello Ted, and yes you may," she got closer to me in five seconds than she had with Steve all night, not that I was tracking every move. "I have heard rumors around that you like me Ted. Would you care to elaborate on these rumors?" She smiled as she spoke, knowing she had just put me in an uncomfortable predicament, which was typical of attractive women.

"The rumors are false. I am actually completely obsessed with you and have a shrine at my house I have made of you that I worship every night." My over indulgence made her laugh, and lightened my current situation. The song over the speakers became slow, and soon we were tightly embraced carrying on a slow dance around the room. Every other person in the room faded away, and for the first time in my life I was truly transcendent.

Hello Mary Ann! I almost screamed across the hall the next day, and the volume of my voice created awkward stares from others, but I honestly didn't even care. Mary Ann acknowledged me, but I had to approach her.

"Hey there," as I said hello, I noticed an abundance of makeup on her right eye, and she turned away from me upon my notice. "What is that? Who did that to you?" The anger building up inside of my body was like a bomb, waiting for the flame.

"It's nothing Ted, please, I have to go to class. As I reached out for her arm, she pulled away and walked with haste to her next class. *This is not over.*

"Mary Ann!" I hurried to catch up with her as she tried to shoo me away.

"Ted, please just leave me alone I have to get home now" she spoke with a whimper in her voice, and adrenaline started to fill my veins.

"Mary Ann, I want to know what happened! If you tell me I will leave you be, I promise." As those words came out of my mouth, I felt a hand pull my shoulder, and a clenched first ripped across my face with a force that broke my nose upon instant contact. I hit the ground, but remained conscious, and stared up at Steve fully flexed out above me. I dove into his mid-section and tackled him onto the ground, and as his fists hit my sides one after another, my awareness of physical pain fell away and I shot up and pummeled my fists into his face. One after another, my fists started to seize his, and soon spectators were pulling me off him and Steve was left lying on the sidewalk completely unconscious. Once my mind realized what had happened, I was overwhelmed with physical, mental and emotional stress, and I blacked out.

My eyes felt like they weighed a ton as my body regained composure, and once I could regain understanding, all I saw was Mary Ann in front of me.

"How are you? Welcome back," her voice comforted every part of me, and I smiled as the pain in the body subsided.

"Steve…" she stopped me before I could finish.

"When we danced at homecoming, I felt a connection. After the dance when we went back to his house I confronted him about our relationship, and broke it off. It was probably a bad idea to provoke a jock that had been drinking, and I received the physical punishment. The only reason I didn't tell you the next day is because I was worried about your well-being, and here I am, dabbing your wounds with a washcloth," as she finished she had a smile on her face, and I couldn't help but smile.

"I am glad I got my chance to give Steve a little piece of my mind Mary Ann, both of us knew he deserved everything I gave him," as I spoke a tear came down from her eye, and she looked away. I reached out for her chin and turned her back towards me, with a tear streaming down from mine.

"Ted I'm just happy you treated me to that dance, it may just have saved my life."

As those words came out of her mouth, the screen went black, and it rose back into the rafters. I couldn't help but look back and feel a presence that I sensed was Mary Ann's, and to be met with the crying eyes of Marilyn. The whole room was silent, and the memories shone before everyone weighed heavy. I couldn't even grasp the gravity of the situation I was in, and the frail girl from before walked back out into the middle of the stage.

"Our jury will meet, and in fifteen minutes' time we will have the decision," she was gliding back before the sentence was done, and everyone in the room got up and walked towards the exits. I was numb, and my eyes yearned for a connection from my Mother's and just as The Hope was walking towards the exit, she turned around and returned my stare with a tear-filled glance of her own.

"Whatever happens, just remember to stay calm Ted." Marilyn's words hit me again like stones, the ability to stay calm had left me hours ago. I turned around and scanned the room again. There was a general bustle going on as people were chatting amongst themselves. Occasionally a stray eye would catch mine, but I was not able to find the set I was truly searching for.

"Who makes up the jury?" Even though my asking of the question was necessary, I deep down didn't even mind to know.

"I have never heard anything about them, Marilyn said, but the same woman who walked out to address us was the one at my trial as well." Her realization came to her the same time as it did to me. Just as I was going to dive deeper, the lights flickered and in came The Circle and the Hope again, and I began to feel an overwhelming anxiety creep around my body as I studied The Hope's body language.

As they sat, the same woman walked out and simply put out both hands to calm and quiet everyone, and she began to speak softly.

"We have come to a decision, and as it stands, we will begin again tomorrow at the same time to move further into the life and transgressions of Ted Wall." She put her hands together and laid them on her stomach, and took a deep breath. It was in that moment where my brain had to remind myself to breathe, and I couldn't remember the last time I took a breath.

"We hereby find Ted Wall guilty of the act of supreme lust, and sentence him to one night in Hell." She turned and walked away silently, and the room was still.

Marilyn got up frantically and put her hands on the sides of my head. "Remember, stay calm, stay stro ," her words fell to black. The room had fallen to black, as I felt a searing pain shoot from the back of my head to my toes, I was gone.

7

As I came to, my eyes couldn't adjust to the darkness that surrounded me. The faint hum outside reminded me of something, but my mind was so shattered I could barely piece my reality together. I did a quick check of myself to make sure I was complete, but the pain that lingered in the back of my head was unbearable. I extended out my arms to all sides, and came to the realization I was inside of something, and I could feel all the sides without even fully extending my arms.

I need to get out of here! My claustrophobia was setting in and I began to hyperventilate. Sweat covered my brow, and my body couldn't remain still. Although there was nothing restricting me, my feet could barely swing forward a foot before hitting the encasement of what I was inside.

Please! At the full brink of my panic settling in, the bottom of the capsule opened, and my body fell. The rush of air around me relieved my claustrophobia but I soon realized that I was in complete free fall. I reached around me and felt no restraint, and no parachute. The panic that was stalled had aggressively returned. I felt like screaming, but I couldn't make a sound. As I looked down, I could see the outline of a road appearing, and what seemed to be streetlights following on the left side.

I am going to die! The thought alone confused me, yet the fear of dying had found a way to resurface. As my body hurled toward the road, I soon made contact. The right side of my body and face took the brunt of the impact, and the feeling of asphalt against my bare skin trumped the previous feelings that preceded. I slowly got up, and was amazed to find no bodily harm, although the discomfort in my head had now swarmed the rest of my body.

"Get up, you'll be fine, we have to go now," said a short man who appeared out of the darkness of the streetlight. He revved an engine of what looked to be a motorcycle, and was out of sight in a flash. As I got up to my feet, I could sense two things. There was a bike up against the lamppost, and down the road away were multiple headlights coming closer by the second. *I have to get out of here!*

My mother never wanted me to own or ride on a motorcycle, because she feared for my life. Ironically here I was, in Hell, going as fast as the bike could take me down a long narrow road, as streetlights zoomed overhead. I secretly learned how to ride from a roommate I had lived with after college, and although I never owned my bike, I snuck out on his every occasionally, for a quick rush. I was catching up to the man who had alarmed me, and behind me the headlights were remaining at a distance. There was no speedometer on the bike, but I knew that this was the fastest I had ever gone, and if one pothole took my front wheel I would be a goner. *There I go again, thinking of death. How ironic! Potholes in Hell; it would be too perfect.* I noticed above us the streetlights began to spread out, and a building was appearing on the left. The bike in front me dove off towards the building and sprayed up gravel as he came to a complete stop.

I didn't even get a word in before he was running in the back door of the establishment, and I did my best to keep up pace behind him.

As we entered the back door we walked directly into a changing room, full of mirrors and make up brushes, yet I couldn't make any proclamations of where we were based on prior experiences. I raced through a door on the opposite side of the room and we walked directly into a strip club. The eerie part about it was even though I saw a DJ and speakers; the whole club was completely silent. There was a large stage in the middle and smaller side stages, but there were no girls to be seen. The stray gentlemen in the club sat, lifeless eyes facing forward, with clenched fists full of money. The man I was following raced to the other side of the club, and began to harass a guy sitting in a booth. I stopped moving towards them, and observed as the lifeless man being thrown around opened his mouth and seemed to speak. I couldn't hear any words, but the second he spoke the man I had been following threw him down, and motioned me to follow him out.

As I began to pick up my pace to follow again, the light went down and out walked a woman. Her head was down and her shoulders were slouched. All at once every guy in the club heads raised and a grin came over their faces. It was at that same moment I recognized the back door being broken down, and multiple people racing into the back of the club. The mystery man I had been following grabbed my arm and violently pulled me towards the front door. As I was just about to exit the building I turned back to the woman on stage and quickly recognized the pair of beautiful green eyes I had been searching for. *Mary Ann.*

I was overcome with emotion, but gunshots rang out and whizzed past me, and the motivation to leave once again returned to me. I didn't even have a second to speak to...*Phil*...I'll just call him that for now, before he was racing away again. I jumpstarted my bike, and once again I was blazing a trail down the dark road. I stayed full throttle until I was beside him, and I began to scream out.

"What was that back there? Who was that guy? Why was Mary Ann on stage? Who is chasing us?" I blurted out questions rapid fire, yet Phil remained eyes forward. It was in that moment where I consciously did what my Mother was always worried what would accidently happen. I swerved my bike in front of his, and for a moment our bikes and both of us were suspended in the air. As we came to a tumbling halt, Phil raced over to me and put his hands around my throat.

"I know you have questions, but if we don't succeed before day break, you will never know the truth, now let's go!" He spoke in a subtle rage, but I didn't doubt he was telling the truth. My frustration lifted, and I returned to my bike and began to follow again.

Calm yourself Ted. Marilyn's voice lingered into my head, and a deep breath followed.

Further down the road the lights again became increasingly further apart, and it became hard to follow anything other than the small red light on the back of Phil's bike. He started to veer off to the left, and my eyes began to register wood panels laid out in front of us. *It's a dock.*

As I looked down to both of my sides as we kept a steady pace, I could not see water, but I could hear the faint sound of water hitting the dock. Phil got off his bike and started walking towards the end. He quickly descended a four-rung ladder into a small boat, and motioned me to get in. *Okay so there is water.* I thought it was best not to ask him any more questions as I got in and he quickly started to row.

Behind me I saw and heard the sound of bikes racing down the dock and what seemed to be four or five large men stalled at the end. Phil had his head turned rowing as fast as he could, and the dock started to fall out of view. Just as I took my first breath in what seemed like hours, I heard a splash behind the boat, and Phil looked back with a look of terror.

The explosion that happened underwater lifted the backside of the boat where I was and I was propelled forward, over Phil and where the oars were. The black water in front of me greeted me like a concrete driveway, and the feeling of cold water overtook my body instantly. As I resurfaced, again I felt a violent pull as Phil was hurrying me through the water, and behind me I could faintly see figures in the water coming towards us. As I began to swim faster and faster through the water I started to feel things underneath me. The feeling of things gliding through my legs began to unsettle me, but the adrenaline was pushing those feelings away. The depth of the water began to change as I started to feel a muddy bottom. Phil was sloshing his way out of the water and I quickly followed. As we raced across a lawn we quickly made our way into what looked like from the outside an old Victorian estate. The estate did not look in the best of shape; the exterior had a worn paint job, and I had to make my way across a minefield of misshapen wood and nails glistening, looking for flesh.

As we made our way in I started to notice people lying all around the house. Every single person I saw lying lifeless on the floor had their eyes wide open, and seemed to be in shock. Phil was hastily making his way around the bottom level, stepping and dodging when need be to make sure he didn't disturb the people laid out all over the floor. As I reached the stairs I started up them, and it seemed as though there were more than normal. My legs started to burn as I rose up the stairs two by two, and finally was welcomed by a landing to the top level of the house. Phil quickly raced down the left hallway and opened all the doors, one by one. I followed and couldn't help but notice the increasing amount of wide-eyed lifeless people lying in the rooms. As Phil kicked down the fourth door, I looked through and did a quick scan of my own. Lying on the opposite side of the room was a frail body with her back up against the wall. I would have kept going if I didn't register the color of the eyes I saw, I didn't know that shade of green from anywhere else.

"Mary Ann!" I slid over to her, and put my hands on her shoulders. She didn't budge as I tried to get her attention, and the look in her eyes was as lost as I felt. Phil raced back in and grabbed my shoulder, and even though I protested, I had to follow him out. My eyes didn't leave hers as I back-pedaled out of the room, and I swore I saw her reach her hand out for me. Physically, emotionally and mentally windswept, I followed Phil as he hit the last door, and quickly went over to greet a hunched over man. The man was deathly skinny, with bones that I could watch shift under his skin as he tried to escape Phil's embrace. The man had an elastic band around his arm and a needle lying next to him lying on the floor, and Phil quickly relieved the man of consciousness with a swift right hook. Phil scanned the area all around the skeleton man, and finally found a vial with a red liquid inside and retrieved it. In that same moment, the sound of footsteps thundered down the hall, and Phil gave me the first look of panic I had seen come from him all night. He embraced me in the form of a strong hug, and put the vial in my hand.

"Take this! It will remain with you after this night is through. Use it to learn the truth, and be ready to embrace the truth after you uncover it. You can only use it once, so make sure it is the right time. All hope is not lost Ted, even in the darkest moments you can find the light, and when you do, all will be known and nothing can live in the shadows any longer." As his words ceased, a figure appeared at the doorway, and Phil pushed me towards an open window on the other side of the room.

As I exited onto an overhang on the front of the house, I looked back and was struck with a feeling in my stomach that paralyzed my senses. *Ted.* I didn't see what he did after I started to retreat to the end of the overhang, but I heard multiple gun shots and what seemed to be a scream ringing out from Phil's mouth, but it quickly became silent. I jumped and did a barrel roll down onto the ground, and with the remaining energy I had I ran as fast as I could in the opposite direction of the water, into an oncoming pasture. Several figures raced after me but I soon picked up my pace as a second wave of adrenaline passed through me. The figures started to fade in the distance as I ran, but before I could stop myself, I ran directly off the side of a cliff that was directly in front of me. As I began a second free fall, the light on the horizon crept in, and I was soon surrounded in it.

8

My eyes opened and I registered a sound coming from the outside of my door. I was laid out on my bed and I quickly realized where I was, and in that moment, I also realized I had a small glass object in my right hand. Before I could put the mental puzzle back together from what just happened the knocking on the door became louder. The second my foot hit the floor soreness overcame me and I braced myself on the wall, and walked gingerly over to the door.

"Oh Ted, you're alright!" Marilyn's hug trumped the feeling of every sore muscle on my body, and the warmth of her touch filled me with life I forgot I had. As our embrace ended, I slid behind her and closed the door and led her over to the couch.

"Marilyn, I saw Mary Ann. She is in hell, and so was Ted," as I spoke Marilyn became frightened and put her hand on mine. "She was there, but I don't know why. I need to get her out of there, and make sure she's alright," Marilyn turned away, and a tear again graced her eye.

"Ted, what you saw wasn't real," both eyes streamed tears down as she tried to help me understand.

"Marilyn, I know what I saw...Look!" I opened my hand and showed Marilyn the vial, and as I did I got the feeling Marilyn knew what it was. "This was given to me last night, and if this is real, where I was and what I saw was real" my words sounded skittish, and Marilyn seemed to not want any of them.

"Come on, you can't be late, the trial starts again soon, meet me downstairs in fifteen minutes." She got up and exited without anything else being said, and a mixture of panic and confusion overcame me.

My body protested getting dressed and making myself presentable, as the yearning for answers bogged me down from the inside out. I opened the door and walked down the hall, and into the lobby. I sat and took deep breaths to try to calm my mind, as my hand once again found its way into my pocket where the vial sat. My eyes found the light in the darkness, as Marilyn reappeared at the top of the stairs and glided in. The sound of the conversations that were around me subsided, and I again felt at peace. She walked over to greet me, and she had the most beautiful gown on, radiating a brilliant shade of green. She walked over to me, winked, and put her hand out.

As we exited again the familiar draft hit me, and as I took a breath in the smell of fresh cut grass ignited my senses. We walked on what seemed to be a shorter path and approached the train station again. The train was already waiting for us as we arrived, and I slowed my pace to a halt. I looked at Marilyn and emotion overcame me. I put my head onto her shoulder, and began to cry. She didn't say anything; she just put her arms around me and rubbed the back of my head. The pain and anxiety that had been building inside of me started to subside, and after a quick wipe of my eyes from Marilyn's scarf, we boarded again.

As we arrived my mind couldn't recall any of the ride, my mind had hit its full capacity for information. We walked through the doors and now instead of being ushered all the way down it was like we had VIP service. I tried to recall all of hell and the magnitude of it, but walking back towards the theater my heart started to beat for the future more than the past. Marilyn hooked her arm around mine and pulled me in close.

"Ted, I have faith today will be a better day for you. I don't know what all went on last night but I am sure whatever happens your will and mental toughness will prove to prevail again." The optimism she emitted was needed, and extremely comforting. I nodded at her kind words, and opened the doors to the theater. As I walked down the seats were about half filled, and the time drew nearer.

I sat and focused on the stage and I saw part of both The Circle and The Hope enter the stage, with the absent ones only being my mother and Ted. *I saw Ted last night,* and as that thought dawned on me he began to walk out onto the stage. *He is coming out of the wrong side.* As the theater filled and the time grew nearer, anxiety started to cloud my senses. *Where is my mother?* The lights in the theater dimmed and the next stage of the trial was set to begin, and there were only seven people on stage. I looked back at Marilyn and all she returned me was the same look of anxiety I had. A short man emerged onto the stage and as he grew closer, a rush of adrenaline ignited my body.

That's the same guy! I met him last night in hell.

He didn't acknowledge me at all before he started to speak. "Hello, and welcome back to the trial of Ted Wall. Yesterday we spoke about Lust, and today the topic of focus is Envy. Some swear it as the most potent cause of unhappiness that exists, and strips us of the enjoyment of solitude. To covet what one does not have does not prove as living, it proves as false imagery. Once again, The Circle will be up first," as he finished two things stung me. First, he didn't acknowledge me but I am sure he was the one with me. Second, my mother was still not there, and as the lights went down and the countdown began, I couldn't help but pray that she was okay.

9

"This party might be the best thing that has ever happened to my life!" That was my friend Mike speaking after he hit the beer bong for the fourth time that night. "You know, with high school ending and going to college next year, I really do feel like I should enjoy myself to the fullest because I know with all of the work that college brings, I won't be able to party that much." He gave me a look after he spoke, and I honestly couldn't tell if he was joking or not.

"Yeah, I'm sure college won't provide any of these opportunities, with so much homework and responsibility." I had to raise my voice over the music blaring from the speakers but I'm sure he understood my blatant sarcasm involved with that statement.

As I walked around the house, the party was slowly taking casualties. I had been to high school parties before, but being at one after graduation felt so gratifying. Lauren's house was huge, and had a multi-level outdoor access to enjoy, so there were people coming and going all night. Mike tapped my shoulder and pointed out a girl across the room, dragging on a cigarette and bobbing her head up and down with the music.

"That's Erica, she's a sophomore at Ohio University, just got into town for her brother's graduation." Mike spoke with a stutter, like he was nervous to even be looking at her across the room.

"But like I said before Mike, with all the homework and stuff in college, girls like that are secondary, and they have to be fit into the college machine." I shot him a smug grin, feeling my alcoholic buzz intensify.

"Ted, good thing we aren't in college yet my friend," he said as he walked over across the room and entered the group she was in, and casually lit a bummed cigarette.

My mind started to wander as I enjoyed the solace of my own company for a moment when I noticed a new group of females walk in. It didn't take me long to meet eyes with someone I unconsciously yearned for since our homecoming breakthrough.

"Well, I didn't know I would be seeing you tonight. If I would have known, I would have dressed up a bit and took more time to get ready." My sarcasm was blatant, as I was known for my laid-back appearance and careless good looks.

"Ted, it truly is a pleasure, and fitting I find you alone in the corner of the room. It's starting to become a routine." What a reply! It caught me off so well I choked on my drink a little bit. As I started my comeback, Mary Ann shuffled away with her friends to get a drink, and I was left alone twice in ten minutes.

I walked out in the backyard on the lowest level and smelled a familiar smell, almost like a skunk was right around the corner. Down by the bonfire I saw Mike sitting with a group that included Erica, and they seemed to be passing around something lit, I decided to investigate.

"Something smells good!" I burst into the circle, right in between Mike and Erica and sat, casually grabbing the joint on the next go around. The conversation was plentiful, but I couldn't help but sense Mike's displeasure in me disconnecting the vibe he had formed with Erica. He got up, mumbled something about the bathroom, and walked back into the house.

"Well, another high school boy here, should have known this is what I was getting myself into." Erica smiled as she spoke, but in the high I was on I didn't know exactly how to reply.

"I just turned nineteen. I am everything a college guy is except for the fact that I'm not in college yet." I smiled back at her, and she shrugged her shoulders.

"I am twenty-one, and being legal not only allows me to drink, but it also puts me out of your league." With those words, she put her hand on my forearm, clenched a bit, and made her way out of the circle.

Even though all hope may have been lost, the liquid and herbal courage running through me had me walking back into the house on a mission. As I made my way around I ran into another familiar face yet again.

"You smell different than when I first saw you tonight Ted." She smiled as she spoke, her eyes focused in on me.

"Mary Ann, you are right. I was out by the bonfire and I seem to have carried the smoke smell inside." She laughed out loud when I said that, and I couldn't help but return the laugh with her.

"Hey, I know this song. Come dance with me Ted," as she grabbed my arm Mike and Erica reappeared on the opposite side of door.

"Teddy, let's go. Erica has a local hook up at the bar down the street, we are leaving now," Mike gave me the look of longing, and Erica winked, because she knew she had a firm grip on my soul in that fleeting moment.

"Mary Ann, I've got to go," it was in that moment I noticed her pure disappointment, but she shrugged me off. She didn't return words as she joined her friends again dancing, never meeting eyes with me again. The walk out the front door and down to the car felt like a muddy trek with my guilt weighing me into the ground, but once I got into the back of the SUV waiting, we were on the road, and the night was still young. Mike passed me back another joint as the driver, who seemed to be one of Erica's friends rolled on blaring music making conversation impossible. Erica had taken the middle seat in the back, and was firmly pressed up against me and started to become more physical.

As the car pulled into the parking lot at the bar, we all exited with a second wind that was ignited by the fresh spring air.

"Just hold on boys, let me go speak with Rob and I will be back." As Erica disappeared into the bar, Mike and I stayed outside, casually watching as people made their way in. Due to my intoxication, I do not know how much time passed, but after what seemed like forever one of Erica's friends came out and lit up a cigarette.

"Hey, do you know where Erica is, I asked. She was going to get us in and she never came back." Her friend shook her head.

"Honey, Erica left about thirty minutes ago. She hit a wall and had to get out of here. She left out the back because she felt bad about leaving you out here, sorry." She turned away and joined some more people smoking and my whole body deflated.

"Can't wait for college, huh?" Mike's sarcasm did not help, and I pulled out my phone to call for a ride home.

As the lights turned back on in the theater the horrible guilt that crept through my body stung like a bee. I turned back to look at Marilyn, and though I saw an anxious sadness in her eyes, she seemed to throw a small smile back at me. *How many guys has she done that to?* I had to laugh at myself, and be reminded that as you grow older you also grow wiser. I tried very hard to suppress that memory, but living it again was as bad as I imagined it would be.

The lights dimmed again, and as The Hope had their chance to redeem me, one question still held my attention. *Where is my mother?*

"Where are we going exactly?" Mary Ann always had to know everything when it came to plans. "Casey and Stephanie invited us out to a Japanese grill, where they cook in front of you. Since you had never done it before I thought it might be fun." She approved of my decision silently, as she often did. As we entered the parking lot we saw their car off in the distance, and slowly rolled up to park next to it. Casey got out and gave us a quick wave, and made his way around to the other side of the car to open Stephanie's door. They kissed as she got out, and greeted us at our car. As we all entered the restaurant a flash came from Stephanie's neck and both Mary Ann and I stopped to take in the sight.

"Well, what do we have here?" Mary Ann grabbed the necklace and examined it with both hands. "What's the occasion Casey, your anniversary isn't for another couple of months?" Casey smiled and turned back at us.

"Just wanted to tell Stephanie that I love her again, and sometimes it comes with material items." Stephanie shrugged a bit, and we were escorted to our table.

The dinner was fun, filled with open flame cooking and the twang of utensils smacking each other as our personal space was violated with flying rice and sake. I couldn't help but notice Mary Ann was fixated on Casey and Stephanie, as they fed each other, and constantly whispered in each other's ears as the dinner rolled along. Mary Ann was becoming a bit unresponsive to my touch, and before I knew it, the meal was over. The ride home that night was silent, and it wasn't too long before both of us were in bed, snoring away. When I awoke in the morning Mary Ann kissed me on the forehead, and left for work after getting ready in the quietest way possible. I couldn't help but feel mentally and emotionally fatigued after the bombardment of physical affection that I watched at the dinner table. I didn't want to hate on their love, but I needed to remind Mary Ann that her affection is all I desire.

"So, where are we going tonight for dinner?" she asked me right on cue as I pulled out of the driveway later that evening.

"Just a little spot downtown I have been meaning to check out for a while now, heard the food is amazing. I smirked as I drove slowly through a roundabout, making a full circle.

Mary Ann didn't even notice where our destination was because she was fixated on her phone. I slowly pulled into our destination and turned off the car, and the confusion set in.

"Ted, we are back in our driveway." She didn't seem amused, but I promised her as I ushered her out of the car I had everything taken care of. As we re-entered the house, a familiar smell hit both of us. I smirked as I walked over the oven and pulled out a pizza I had put in right as we had left. I poured both of us some red wine, and sat her down at the table as I turned on some music. As John Mayer serenaded us, Mary Ann broke her silence.

"Ted, what is this? Why did we get all dressed up for this?" She had a good reason to question me, but as she raised her concerns, I grabbed her hand and led a slow dance in the living room. Although it took a minute, she finally just sank into my arms.

"Mary Ann, even though I might not show in a materialistic way, or by constant physical attention, just understand something, I love you always and forever, no matter what," I had just got that last words out of my mouth before she kissed me, and the whole world melted away.

As the lights came back on, I was feeling emotion heavier than ever. As I wiped my tears from my face, a figure had appeared in my vision that made my heart race again. My mother was back on stage, and she sat up with a purpose. Even though the main question on my mind was where had she been, it was so nice to see that she was back again. The lights remained on, and I knew that in just minutes time a verdict would send me somewhere, and the anxiety of Hell raced back into me.

I turned back at Marilyn, and I could tell her mind was racing on a tangent, and she comforted me instantly, as she only could.

“Such a hopeless romantic Ted! It’s so sweet to see. Nothing gets me more than the love a man has for a woman. It trumps everything.” She leaned over and kissed me on the cheek, and my body seized. I closed my eyes with her touch, and the lights dimmed again, and the small familiar shadow of a man made his way back out.

“We hereby find Ted innocent of the supreme sin of Envy, and grant him a night in Heaven.” His eyes met mine and seemed to pass along a sense of hope, and as I felt a pair of hands on my shoulders, the world around me just simply faded away.

10

As my eyes lifted again, I found myself in what seemed to be a middle school gymnasium. The area around me was filled with people, and the woman next to me grabbed my forearm and motioned her finger to her mouth to have me stay quiet. On the stage were two young children, with the young girl lying over the boy, as she rose, she just simply gasped, choked, and fell onto the bed next to the boy. The whole room applauded as both children got up and took a bow, and a makeshift curtain on both ends of the stage closed the stage off from the crowd, as the lights came back on. I looked at the woman next to me, and she met my gaze with two misty eyes.

"Hello Ted, it's nice to meet you, I have heard wonderful things about you! Let's take a walk." As she finished she seemed to cry a bit more.

"You can use my sleeve if you want to," I said as I extended out my arm and she just smiled back at me.

"Shakespeare always gets me, I can't help it," she spoke as we entered the cold night atmosphere, and my lungs lit up.

"Excuse me, what is your name, if I may ask?" I was determined to learn more about my surroundings after the hellish race I experienced a night before.

"Yes, sorry, my name is Evelyn. Welcome to heaven," she said as she smiled and hugged me, and continued walking.

"So, Evelyn, where are we?" I continued to prod.

"We are in a town right outside of Boston, and that beautiful Juliet on stage was my daughter." She smiled again as she looked back at me, seemingly filled with pride.

"Where are you going now Evelyn? You seem to be in a hurry." I couldn't help but call out the pace she seemed to keep.

"Oh yeah, I'm sorry, just have a couple of stops to make, just wanted to make a quick pit stop," I was confused, but my mind was enjoying the fact I wasn't being chased.

As we walked down the sidewalk adjacent to the school we just exited, the scenery around us changed quickly, and a quick bout of motion sickness settled in. As we made our way down the sidewalk we made up ground quickly to a larger, more modern building.

"Hey, Evelyn, I recognize this building coming up here on the right," I got a rush walking up to what looked like my old dormitory.

As she heard me, she waved me over to follow her, and with a blink of an eye we were inside. As we made our way down the hall, we made our way to my old room. She looked back at me and smiled, and opened the locked door with ease. We entered the room, but the room was empty.

"This is incredible Evelyn, this is my old room. Yet, everything that used to be in here is gone, and no one is around."

Evelyn looked out the window, and smiled back at me. "Come on, we have a couple more places to see," as she started back towards the door she brushed shoulders with me, and when our bodies made contact we were back outside.

"Evelyn, where are we now?" My voice stung a bit as the cold air hit my throat.

"Follow me, quick!" She started into a slight jog as we were running towards what looked like my house, sitting there empty, just as I had believed to have left it. I had a hard time remembering it though, as she opened the front door and made her way in. She walked all the way in, and as she made it to the kitchen she turned around and finally asked me about my current predicament.

"Do you know where you are?" She just simply leaned against the kitchen counter and looked at me.

"Yes, this is my house in Ohio; the house Mary Ann and I lived in. Emotion started to overcome me, but I kept it together.

"Do you notice anything in particular?" Her quiz started to annoy me, but I played along.

"The only thing I can notice right now is that the house is empty, and the house and neighborhood is void of any activity, any life." The answer seemed to suffice for Evelyn, as she started walking out of the front door. The second my foot hit the front porch, the scenery shifted again.

Evelyn was already about ten steps ahead of me as I regained my sense of balance, and I ran to her and grabbed her shoulder.

"Evelyn, please tell me what we are doing." She could sense the sincerity in my voice, and just smiled and waved me inside. The facility we were entering was an old dive Mary Ann and I went to when we first dated, and the interior hadn't changed a bit. Yet as I walked in, the people that were in the bar was just a bit different. Evelyn walked over to the end of the bar and faced the stage on the other side of the room, and hooked my arm with hers as Leroi Moore walked out onto the stage; solo, holding only a saxophone. Hiding behind a very familiar pair of sunglasses, he began to play the most beautiful rendition of 'Somewhere Over the Rainbow' that my ears ever had the pleasure of hearing. An involuntary tear came to me eye, and Evelyn shuffled us over to a booth. As he continued to play, a musical coma overcame me, and I was on life support. I closed my eyes, and as I opened them after a prolonged closure I started to notice the people in the bar surrounding me.

Alan Rickman, Freddie Mercury, Richard Wright, some of my favorite people.

As my excitement of my surroundings flooded my thoughts, the lights went down. Leroi left the stage, and a soft mist started to rise from the sides of the stage. Just as I looked over to Evelyn the first note of 'Purple Rain' started, and a small figure donned the stage.

"Ted, you have to know something," Evelyn's words floated on the melody, and I began to sink. "In heaven, there are things you can't control, and there are things you can control." The past, although enticing to think about and act on, is the past. No matter what your intentions are, the past is gone, and it will never be able to be experienced again. Yet, the ones who have passed on are able to choose to live on, as great deeds in one life lead to a second chance in another," I became transfixed on what she was saying, trying to piece it together.

"Heaven is among the living Ted, as everything that can be wished for can be manifested here, and although we take different forms and have to adjust to life on earth again, life goes on through us," I stared into her eyes, as she smiled and took in the music and a sip of her drink in hand.

"Ted, if ultimately you make it to heaven, your soul will pass on. The living take on the souls of the deceased, and the experiences on earth begin again. Great musicians that passed on joined great living musicians, and their energy could resonate again. You can see the same lying in the words of a great novelist, the strokes of a great artist, and the power and elegance of a supreme athlete."

Her words took a while to digest, but as they began to settle I felt a new hope, a hope I hadn't felt since my realization overcame me.

"Evelyn, I am truly taken by your words and your enlightenment of the truth, but I have just one question for you. If heaven allows re-entrance to the living world, why didn't my mother move on? Evelyn kept her eyes closed as the music and smiled at my question, then grinned at me.

"Ted, since the moment her life was taken she expressed but one thing…to defend you, whenever that day may come." She finished speaking; she put her hand on top of mine, and hummed along to the sound of the music flowing around us. I closed my eyes, and when I opened them, again I found myself lying in my bed.

11

The optimism that resonated in my body as I awoke was intoxicating, my senses felt heightened, and my reasoning seemed as sharp as it had ever been. Evelyn's words of enlightenment had a way of setting my mind on fire, and I yearned for more information about the lighter side of heaven. I sat on the edge of my bed, running my hands up and down my legs, gently massaging my muscles that had just a night ago been to hell and back, and reminded me with every step the next day. I perked up as a knock came on the door, and without even checking the peep hole I swung the door open, and embraced Marilyn.

"Well, what a difference one night makes," she exclaimed as I smiled back at her.

"Marilyn, I have to tell you about last night! The feeling of hope has rejoined me, and I couldn't feel better!" As I spoke she walked over to the couch, sat down and put out her hand allowing me to continue.

"This woman named Evelyn took me all around, and she told me souls live on! I watched Leroi Moore serenade a crowd on his saxophone, and then Prince came out and brought the house down like he always had when he was alive. She also said that souls have the ability to live on, and we can live on in the form of others, and it just makes me wonder about how the living will progress. With the overwhelming amount of energy being passed onto the living, the future is a bright one. I feel as though someone like Prince was a culmination of dozens of musicians molded together, and someone like him wasn't even possible a hundred years ago because he had to be built. I want to heighten the next generation, I want to help, and I want to return." I finished my soliloquy as Marilyn got up and hugged me, and she once again had tears in her eyes.

"Tears of happiness I hope," I said as I wiped them away.

"We have to get ready Ted, I'll meet you downstairs in thirty." She exited the room, and left me a bit anxious, the whole time I was in heaven I couldn't wait to tell her what I had learned.

As I got out of the shower, I looked into the mirror. *My physical form, as much energy I have put into it, kind of ironic that all I wish now is to be lifted from it.* I wasn't an opposing body, standing a shade over five foot ten. I had a little bit of grey peeking through, and the retained facial hair in a groomed sense since I was in college, just completed my look. As I straightened my tie, I took a deep breath and stared back at myself.

You look good, you feel good, cherish this moment! I swung the door opened and had a spring in my step as I walked down into the lobby, I sat down on a bench without the need of energy from food, I was alive today. I found my hand nervously tapping my knees as I sat and waited to leave again. It was amazing as my eyes lifted; the way Marilyn controlled a room as she walked through it. The violet dress she donned glimmered and with each step she exuded confidence unmatched in my eyes.

As we walked out towards the train, I couldn't help but notice the difference in the landscape around us. The most beautiful gardens surrounded us, and the smell of the fresh foliage was all around. We made our way onto the train, and sat down by ourselves.

"Marilyn, with the knowledge of heaven and its ability to extend existence, I won't lie, I have a renewed sense of being. I have my sights set on something, and I am truly excited about it." I looked at her, and she threw me back a look that melted me, as it always had.

"I couldn't be happier Ted. That realization is truly one to marvel at, and Evelyn sounds like an amazing person you got to meet." The look in her eyes drowned me, and she looked ahead again. As the train began to slow, I grabbed her hand and led the march on. I was going to move on through this world, I was going to exist again, I was going to win.

As we entered the building again, I didn't even acknowledge anyone on our trek to the theater, and as we entered the room it looked as though we were a bit early. The theater sat empty. I looked back at Marilyn and shot her an anxious glance, but nothing was taking me off the high I had woken up on today. I sat, and again found myself tapping my knee, and closed my eyes and starting humming again, I kind of fell into a daze but snapped out of it as the lights dimmed, and when I opened my eyes I watched a man walk out from the back side of the stage. He was about to address everyone, yet I realized something, *where is everyone?* No one from The Hope or The Circle was on stage, and as I slowly turned my head back and looked at the seats behind me there was no one to be seen, even Marilyn.

Where is she? What is going on? As I frantically conjured up questions in my head I was stilled by the address of the man on stage in front of me.

"Hello, and welcome back to the trial of Ted Wall. Today we speak about Pride, as some might say the foremost of all of the deadly sins." As the figure spoke, he had his hands folded behind his back, looking straight ahead. He didn't even seem to notice no one was there, and before I could investigate further, the screen dropped down and I was immersed once again.

12

"Mary Ann, I really do think green is your color, and I think we should match it up for this weekend," we went through different color examples as we prepared for prom.

"I know Ted, but your color is blue, so we are going to have to come to an agreement here or this won't work," as she walked over to me with the blue color patch, she put it up against my head, compared it with my eyes, and kissed me. "You are the boss, whatever you want to wear I will for you, color choice has never been my strong suit,"

I threw all the color patches on the ground, and laid down on my bed.

"You know, ever since the moment we danced at homecoming I have been waiting to publically dance with you again, and I am glad we have been able to privately practice over the past couple of months." She grabbed me off my bed, and dragged me around the room. As Coldplay serenaded us we made our way around my hardwood floors.

"Hey Ted, got a minute?" Patrick shouted at me, and I quickly made my way back to him in the hallway.

"What is up my friend?" The amount of confidence I exuded after starting to date Mary Ann was exorbitant, and even casual conversation held true.

"Ted, is there any way I could stop over after school and talk about a couple of things?" The look in his eyes looked serious, and I quickly nodded and accepted his self-invitation.

"Mary Ann and I will be at my house around five. Come over any time after that." Patrick smiled, patted me on my shoulder, and walked away.

"He will probably be here soon, I wonder what he has going on?" Mary Ann returned my confusion in her glance back at me, but there was no worry in the room. I heard the door downstairs swing open and a quick hello exchanged, as footsteps made their way up.

"Hello there!" Patrick walked over and hugged Mary Ann, threw his book bag down and sat down Indian style on my bedroom floor.

"Ted, Mary Ann, thanks for having me over, you two have always been so nice to me, and if there was anyone to talk to, it would be you two."

While Patrick shuffled his things around, I looked at Mary Ann with a perplexed look.

"Prom is right around the corner, and it has been a tough time for me. Over the last two years or so things have changed for me, and it has been kind of an uphill battle to mentally tackle. Everyone has been asking me about prom, and I felt like after enough time, this would be the perfect time to clear things up." Patrick looked at us, and my look hadn't changed. Mary Ann had the same confused look on her face.

"I'm sorry, it's like me to beat around the bush. It just happens, what I am trying to say is, I'm gay, and just being able to admit it to myself and to close friends is such a relief, and I am ready to have it known to the world," Patrick finished with a tear and a smile.

Mary Ann rushed across the room to embrace him, and I joined in on a group hug, and as Patrick returned our embrace, I could sense relief and a couple tears coming down.

"Well, now that's out, I truly feel better," Patrick fist pumped, and laid back on my floor. "Were you able to get any suitors for prom?" Mary Ann pried, riding the moment. He sat back up, and just simply shook his head, throwing us a sense of disappointment and carelessness that fit the moment.

"Unfortunately, no, but I have come to the realization that going alone would serve me well, and would prove to be the best-case scenario." Patrick jumped up, and saluted us with misty eyes, and bid us farewell on that note.

The emotion of this after school encounter had overtaken me, and for the rest of the day my mind wandered, and the sense of happiness I felt for Patrick trumped thc night.

"Ted, can I talk to you?" Whenever Mary Ann said that it always scared me, like something completely morbid was arising.

"What is it Mary Ann, what's the problem?" She had her head rested on my chest and looked back at me. "I think you should go to prom with Patrick," and as she spoke, she smiled back at me with puppy dog eyes.

"Mary Ann, we have spent countless hours picking out colors and matching wardrobes, and now I am going with someone that is not you?" My protest did not stand up long.

"Patrick needs you, and it may just be one night that will change his life, as you have the rest of yours to change mine," as she spoke she leaned back and kissed me, all but engraving the decision into existence.

The gymnasium that held our prom was lit up like a Hollywood premiere, and you could hear the music pumping from three blocks down. As I exited the limousine, Mary Ann smiled at me as I made my way towards the front doors. As I approached the front door, I looked over at Patrick and smiled. He had a blue bow tie and a jet-black suit, and he did look good. As we checked in, we took the steps down, and as we approached the perimeter of the dance floor, I looked back at him, and put his hand in mine, and entered, with either one of us ever looking back.

The lights lit up in the theater, and as I regained a sense of my surroundings I became alarmed, but didn't have much time as the figure made his way back onto the stage again. As I looked ahead on stage, there was no one representing The Circle on the left side of the stage, but I had two sets of eyes looking back at me from The Hope's side, my mother and Marilyn's. As I tried to relay anything I could to them, the theater became black, and the countdown began again.

"I am going to miss you Ted, I really am," Mary Ann hugged me, and I could feel a soft whimper on my shoulder.

"We will be able to see each other in a couple of weeks, you won't have enough time to miss me before I'll be right back in your arms," I said soothingly. She seemed to find solace in this statement, as she began to walk away from me. It wasn't easy to be away, but my mother had asked me to stay for a summer term at college, and Mary Ann was heading back to Ohio to work with her cousin.

"With technology today Mary Ann, we can not only speak to each other every day, we can see each other too." Mary Ann nodded as she understood our predicament, kissed me, and made her way to her friend's car. I told her to message me when she got to the airport, and even though it was only a ten-minute drive to the gate it felt like days before I heard from her again.

"I know mom, but I won't be missing much school, and I know it would mean the world to Mary Ann." My mother was always my voice of reason, but love was always the trump card that seemed to battle reason.

"You have only been away from each other for three weeks Ted, and I would say if you are going to travel across the country to see her, I would at least let her know you were on your way." Her words were heard, but not registered. The warmth of Mary Ann's touch drove my adolescent mind, and being away from it drained me, and needed to be revived.

"Mom, the second I get back to Ohio, I will stop by Mary Ann's house then I will come see you, I promise." Mom had a soft spot for our meetings, and she gave me the go ahead to make travel plans.

It seemed like every time I deplaned in Ohio there was some sort of weather situation to deal with, and on this summer night a warm front had brought in a severe bout of thunderstorms that made my drive a bit more hectic than imagined. As much as I wanted to drive straight to my mother, the directions I had programmed were leading me straight to Mary Ann, and I was only fifteen minutes away as I hit the highway. The second I turned onto her street, I got the same rush that I felt when we first met, and I was so excited to see her. I pulled up and parked on the street, yet due to the darkness and the rain pouring down, I couldn't see anything in my nearby surroundings. I snuck over the to the side of the house that I had met her at years ago, when it required me to sneak out of my house late at night just to see her. I became completely drenched as I hurried over to find shelter by a low hanging tree that sat up against the window, and raised myself up to peer into the living room. As I looked inside, every single cell in my body seized and my mind went blank as I saw Mary Ann sitting, and on the other side of the room sat Steve, and they seemed to be in the middle of deep conversation.

As I sat outside becoming more and more drenched with the rain falling, I couldn't take my eyes off the sight that was inside the house. Mary Ann and Steve stayed in what seemed like a hot exchange of words, and it wasn't until the end of the conversation that I saw the first physical exchange. Steve got up and walked over to Mary Ann, as tears streamed down her face, Steve grabbed both sides of her head and pulled her in for a kiss, and although I turned away because of a sound manifesting itself behind me, it appears Mary Ann returned it. The front door swung open and I could hear Steve's footsteps on the front porch, and they began to slosh their way across the front yard to his car. The internal struggle was raging inside me of whether to go inside and face Mary Ann, and ultimately solace overcame and I returned unnoticed to my car, and was on my way.

"Ted! There you are," my mother grabbed me and held me like I was coming back from war, and deep down it felt as though I had.

"Hello mom, I missed you," I kissed her cheek, and made my way upstairs to rid myself of my wet clothing and recent onslaught of the scene I had witnessed. The darkness outside gave way to first light, yet my mind hadn't even let itself fully rest. As my mother crept in to wake me up, she seemed to notice my restlessness as she tugged at my shoulder and invited me down for breakfast. The image of Steve kissing Mary Ann haunted my reality, and I knew that I wouldn't be able to live the day without confronting her.

"Ted honey, is there something that you want to talk about?" my mother always had a way of knowing, but I couldn't bring it up to her.

"No, I just have to go see Mary Ann soon. I wasn't able to see her last night." I looked away when I proclaimed this knowledge, and instantly my mother could tell of the difficulty that was awaiting me in this day, but remained silent.

I rang the doorbell at Mary Ann's house with hesitance, and the second it rang my heart seemed to seize in my chest, and my breathing became inconsistent. When the door opened Mary Ann involuntarily leapt into my arms, and I returned the gesture the best I could.

"What are you doing here?" she kissed me and took me inside, and before I knew it I was in the same spot as Steve had been just twelve hours before.

"I had to come back for a couple days and I thought a surprise was in order." She sat up straight and smiled at me, and I could tell she genuinely cared that I was there.

"Oh, I am so happy you are here, it has been so boring here, and I have missed you so much!" She ran her hands through her hair, but I couldn't return any physical contact, my senses were still under control of the memory I had from the night before.

"I don't think someone like you could be bored for too long," I said. She became instantly alert.

"Ted, what do you mean?" she shot a glance back at me that meant business.

"No I am just saying that you never seem to be alone for too long, you always have something going on," I was five feet deep and was continuing to dig as she sat up even straighter, not amused at all by my first two sentences I had for her.

"Ted, what are you talking about?" She just stared back at me, and my mind had no filter in the one moment I wish it would.

"I wanted to surprise you last night, but when I approached your door, I was reluctant to enter because I heard and saw a familiar face and voice." When I mentioned the truth, she rolled her eyes and threw her hands in the air.

"Ted, come on. Are we really bringing this back up? Steve and I are done, and we have been done for a good time now." She had a way of asserting herself that paralyzed my reason, but I was ready with defense.

"So how do you explain the kiss last night? It seemed like you enjoyed it from my vantage point." As those words left my mouth, I realized I had revealed myself, and I was now six feet deep.

"You came home and sat outside my house and spied on me? And now as you sit in here you are prosecuting me with this information? Do you want to know my side of the equation or does it even matter to you?" Her questions pierced right through me; my defenses were down.

"No explanation is needed. I just know if the feelings still exist between you two, last night was all I needed to know the truth." She shook her head and chuckled as I expressed my thoughts, which began to frustrate me even more.

"Steve came over to seek and complete closure on what we once had, as we did end our relationship rather suddenly." Her explanation meant nothing to me; the heat of the moment has blinded my reason.

"So, when he is sober he regains his sense of understanding and becomes compassionate to your feelings; that's how it works?" Bringing back the memory of the physical pain Mary Ann had suffered didn't bode well, and the dirt of my six-foot hole was now burying me.

"Ted, I think you need to leave," she said as tears streamed down her face, and before I could even find the words to rebut her command, I found myself on the outside of the house. When I got back in my car, I began to scream. I yelled, I slammed my fist into my steering wheel, and the only thing that kept me restrained was my seat belt. I put the car in drive, and made my way back to my mother's house.

As I entered my mother's house, she greeted me right away. My frustration led me right past her, and she yelled out to me.

"Ted, stop, what is wrong?" Her concern was sincere, and as I turned back around tears entered my face and I threw myself into her arms. "Mary Ann and I are over mom, I messed it up bad." As I confessed my overreaction, my mom just simply put her arms around me and rubbed the back of my head.

"Maybe it is for the best." Her words were so simple and thought out, and I looked back at her with tear strewn eyes.

"I think so, mom."

As the lights in the theater lit up again, I couldn't help but realize tears were running down my cheeks, as that memory came to light again. My mind was tricky, and had its way of suppressing memories that I had worked so hard to bury as deep as I possibly could. In what seemed like seconds going by and before I could fully recover, the same man was making his way to the middle of the stage, and again he was only joined on stage by Marilyn on the left and my mother on the right.

"We hereby find Ted Wall guilty of the supreme display of the sin of Pride, and sentence him to one night in hell." As his words rang out, my mind couldn't grasp the haste, with no inkling of deliberation on the jury's part, my fate was again decided. My eyes met Marilyn's, and she showed a sense of fright as she put her hand out towards me, with one finger directing itself behind me. I shuffled in my chair, turned my head and saw Ted, staring back at me with deep, lifeless black eyes. As my glare met his, my world once again became black, and the world around me disappeared.

13

When I could come back to reality, my eyes could not paint any picture of my surroundings at all. Even with my eyes wide open, the whole space around me was completely pitch black. As I went to lift my hands to my face, I felt a strain on both of my wrists that were bound to the wall with chains. I struggled a bit, but to no avail. My hands couldn't reach any higher than my waist.

I'm trapped! I could sense I was fully clothed, but the area surrounding me was moist; I could feel it on my skin and I breathed in the moisture with every breath. I had no way to tell time at all, and what felt like a good fifteen minutes went by, and I found myself sitting on the damp floor to alleviate some of the weighted feeling on my legs. As my body started to sink into the ground, I felt a slight release on my wrists. As the feeling shifted, I was able to get my hands to my face, and I rubbed my temples and threw my hands thorough my hair, to regain sense of the topmost extremities. As my hands were caressing life into my head, I began to feel the air in the room thin out. I put my hand back to boost myself off the floor, and as I stumbled forward a bit, my forehead hit a wall in front of me. My feet shuffled underneath me, and as I had my right foot extended, it felt something that set in an instant panic. *The walls are closing in on me.*

I started to jab at the air instead of breathing it in, and panic seized my body. I reached over to my left hand with my right and tried to pry my hand out of the cuff it was clamped in, but I was not able to pry it free. I still was not able to see the walls around me, but I began to feel all four of them as I shuffled my feet around me. I decided to stand tall, and become still to ease my heart and my breathing. The walls on my sides touched my arms, and as I pulled them in front of me the walls started to press against my shoulders and pinned my arms in. The walls in front and behind me got the point where I had about six to eight inches to move my head back and forth, and my mind eased at the idea that my fate was completely out of my hands now. I closed my eyes, and took deep breath after deep breath, calming my nerves and steadying my pulse. Just as I calmed myself down, I heard a trickle to my bottom right side, which I instantly moved my head to look down, but the wall imposing itself in front of me met my forehead. I felt a cold sensation hit my ankles, and my brain could only sense one thing making its way in. *Water.*

The area was so tight, that the water level was at my knees in about a minute, and steadily rising. As I pulled with my arms to try to break free, I realized the inevitable was coming, and it was going to be here soon. As the water broke my waist I started to gasp at air, making sure my lungs knew I was thinking of them as panic ravaged every other part of my body. Before I knew it, my head was the only part of my body not fully submerged with water, and I was taking final breaths. I exhaled and took a heavy breath in, and my body was soon fully under water. If I could pin point how long I held my breath, I would say adrenaline kicked in after ninety seconds, but depravation settled in and I took my first inhale of pure water.

As my lungs filled with water, my mind became drowsy and because I couldn't see anything around me, the other four senses shut down one by one. The last sense I could remember was sound, trying to hear any hope that may be alive. Then, blackness overcame my being again.

Just as my senses had gone away one by one, they started to come back one by one, as I could first feel cold hands on my skin. A deep, sewage odor hit my nose, and stale water swept past my taste buds as I violently tried to replace the saturated areas with clean air. My eyes once again drew in light, and the outline of a figure hovering over me, constantly looking down at me and over his left shoulder. Just as my hearing returned to me I could hear my gasps as they became less muffled, but the figure quickly covered my mouth with his hand.

"I am happy you are able to breathe again, but you have to do so quietly," he whispered so closely to my ear I felt his lips. "We have to go Ted, let me help you up." He pulled my shoulders forward, as I tried to get my bearings before I took one step.

"What is your name, I need to know, I need to remember," I pleaded with him, as the last able body never told me his name, and he sacrificed himself staying with my memories as 'Phil'.

"My name is Michael, and please, we have to go," he pulled me up, and we began to run.

Although I could not see very well, I could now piece together my surroundings a bit better than before. With the curved feeling of the surface I was running on, I concluded quickly that I was in a sewer of some sort, and there was a steady flow of water running against us.

"Where are we going?" When I threw the question out, Michael did not even bother to look back. He picked up the pace, and soon got to a long, vertical ladder running up what seemed like a hundred feet.

"Quickly!" He climbed, one foot over another. I was still trying to make sure all five senses were aligned as I hurried up behind him, and I made the mistake I unfortunately knew I would.

Why did you look down Ted? As I looked back up Michael was now a good portion above me, and I hurried to make up ground. I was about fifteen rungs away from being at the top, and I felt my left foot slip off the rung, and my whole body fell back. My right hand clung onto the ladder and I felt a jolt run through my right arm as it bore all my weight. As I yelled out, Michael slid down and grabbed my left hand and raised me up again. With his body language, I was reminded of two things. *Be quiet, and hurry up!*

The top of the ladder exited into what looked like a prison, or maybe even a hospital with the way the rooms extended out in both directions only spaced out by about ten feet each. The only light I could sense was a low glimmer from lights hung above, and they were spaced out by about thirty feet each. As I kept pace with Michael in front of me, I started to sense something on each side of me. It was hard to fully see, but as the rooms and lights met, I started to see eyes. They followed me down the hall, and every once in a while, a hand joined the set of eyes, pressed up against glass, slowly making patterns in the condensation from the heavy breathing on the other side.

Michael ran past hundreds of doors, and finally came to the end of the hallway. "I cannot stress enough for you Ted, you have to remain silent, and you have to stay by my side." He demanded the same of me as Phil had, and after disobeying once, I wasn't really feeling insubordinate anymore.

We entered another hallway, completely void of rooms that seemed to lead to nowhere. Michael grabbed my hand and led me over the left side, and he started to feel for the wall in front of him. As we walked the walls started to tighten again, and soon we had to shimmy through with our feet sideways, and we were soon granted relief with a small opening. Michael took a deep breath, and put his hand on my shoulder and pushed me down, and soon we were both on our knees facing a dark wall.

"No words Ted, not one," he warned me again, as he slid a small sliver of wood away from the wall, there was a tiny opening, and as my eyesight peered through, my heart raced, and my stomach dropped.

The vantage point I had, made the conversation barely audible, but I saw Vlad, Adolf and Joseph sitting around a table, seeming to be in a heated discussion, and drinking a very dark liquid in short, polished glasses. My eyes went over to Michael's, but his stayed staring forward, not even pausing for a moment to blink. As I looked back, I saw three figures enter the room, and it took everything in my body to keep from going into complete shock, and dropping into a complete panic yet again.

The first figure was one I recognized, but only recently. It was the same man that had presented Pride at my trial, just a day ago. He seemed to be in a good mood, even donning a smile on his face while the second figure entering the room looked to be in pain, and not able to fully keep his motor skills about him. *That's Phil.* It took me a second to fully recognize him, but despite his disheveled appearance I could fully know that it was he, and following him in the room was the one man that seemed to only manifest himself at the darkest of times. *Ted.*

My eyes felt a slight sting settle in as I realized I hadn't blinked in minutes, and my throat strained as I swallowed in unison. I was trying to make out anything I could, but I couldn't hear anything well enough, as they sat and bickered back and forth. As the conversation rambled on, The Circle didn't move, but Phil and the man from my trial started to direct conversation at each other, as they circled the table where the other four were sitting and sipping. As the man from my trial stopped and directed words at Phil, Ted stood up and put his arm around the man from the trial. They showed great concern with Phil, and soon began to retreat towards the door. As he was back stepping, the door slammed, and panic settled in for him. Ted walked over, and picked him up effortlessly, and the other four just watched on. After a couple of words, Ted threw Phil across the room in our direction, and the crunch of bones on the ground as he hit rattled my core. As he struggled to sit up he raised himself, with one gasp of life he reached out in our direction, and softly whispered "*Michael*", and as my wide eyes looked over at Michael, he simply replied "*Gabriel*" before he was once again thrown across the room.

Ted's glance met mine before Gabriel had even hit the other side of the room. I didn't need Michael's encouragement this time; I knew it was once again time to retreat. As I returned to my feet, I felt for a moment a long nail slide down my right arm as I was re-gaining footing underneath myself, and pain seared through my body. Michael was pushing me with his body as we shuffled through the tight hallway, and as we exited we opened the door in front of us, and once again looked out at the dozens of lights and rooms in front of us. I ran as fast as I could, and didn't even really know where I was going. The only thing I knew was that he was gaining on me, as he always had. The eyes again appeared to my sides, and now I could hear moaning and screaming and pleading flooding the hallway, and it began to strain me mentally. *Keep going*!

We continued to run until we finally reached an intersection, and Michael quickly directed me to the right as we started to run again. Now on my sides rooms that had doors had become bars, and hands reached out towards me and the pleading became even more audible. I started to slow, and soon found myself in front of a young boy, whose eyes looked like endless pools of regret, and I embraced him. His sorrow radiated itself through our touch, and Michael was quick to break our connection.

"They are murderers Ted, not even I can save them now," his concern struck heavy, and without any more said, I was running again. We soon found ourselves at another hole in the ground, and we once again started down a ladder. Michael had me go first, and I began to go down two by two as my feet and hands moved quicker than my brain.

My feet hit water, and I was again running as fast as I could. It seemed like just minutes since I was inhaling my last breath, and now I couldn't catch one if my life depended on it. As we made our way down the sewer pipe, I soon noticed a faint hint of light appearing, and started to hear a singular pair of footsteps racing behind us. As we hit the end of the pipe, the drop off was significant. I hesitated to jump, as I yearned for any other information Michael had for me before this night was over. Yet to my surprise, I found Michael and the man from my trial face-to-face about twenty feet back.

"Michael, you have to understand, he is ours," the man stared back at Michael with such anger and hatred I could see it radiating around him.

"I won't let it happen, not this time!" Michael threw out a kick and hit him right in the stomach, and as he doubled over, Michael turned around and b-lined himself towards me, grabbed me and dove off the end of the pipe, and as free fall settled in, the world once again faded away.

14

My eyes opened slowly, and as my first breath entered my lungs, the surroundings sprang hope with their familiarity, and a smile and a tear came to my face at the same time. My mind raced with thoughts of the night before, but being away from it was an instant relief, and my body soon became mobile again as I heard a knock on my door. I glided over to the door, and felt a sense of warmth as I saw Marilyn through the peephole. As my hand reached out for the door handle, I felt a sharp pain radiate through my arm. I lifted up and saw a long, black and red scratch that had spread out. As I recoiled back my right arm, I reached out my left hand and pulled the door back.

All the air that was in my lungs and in the room quickly vacated as the figure in front of me was not a small, graceful beautiful creature. The mixture of fright, anxiety and panic that mixed in my body stopped my heart for a quick instance as the tall, dark eyed man walked past me into my room.

"I am truly intrigued by you Ted. This trial has really become an interesting one, and in my time of doing what I do, I am excited to see how this all turns out."

I didn't say a word, I just watched him walk around my room and slide his finger along things.

"Do you feel worried about the outcome of this trial Ted?" as he asked he peered deep into my soul, as his hands fingered through the collection of music on the other side of the room.

"If I am being honest, I don't want you to know how I feel about this trial, of anything else that has happened since I have been here."

He smiled back at me with a smug sense of happiness, and pulled out a record. As the needle hit, Jim Morrison lit up the room. He walked back over towards me, and stood closer to me than I would have liked.

"Ted, let me give you something to contemplate, if I may." He closed his eyes and nodded his head with the music as he spoke. "I will call off the trial right now, and grant you heaven, with one stipulation," right as the song ended he opened his eyes and glared over at me. "You are awarded heaven, and we get Mary Ann."

He didn't let me answer during my minute or so of silence, because before he even had asked me the question I'm sure he knew what my reaction would be. He just leisurely walked towards the door and grabbed the handle, and turned back one final time.

"You know Ted, it is just something to have in your back pocket; offer stands," and with that he closed the door.

I must talk to Mary Ann, somehow someway! My mind couldn't let the images go, and how cold the room had become, and how strained the air was as he left. I quickly got dressed, and exited the room letting Jim play on.

As I walked to the lobby, I realized that after my conversation with Ted, I was running behind with the trial, and had to hurry to the train station. As I hit the outside walkway I realized something. *Where is Marilyn?* I went back into the lobby and looked around, and eventually made my way back outside where the anxiety of solace had lifted. As I slowly made my way to the train, I was welcomed with a sight for extremely sore eyes.

"Ted!" Marilyn hopped off the train and ran over to me, her yellow dress fluttering in the breeze, with the smell of citrus following her right into my arms. As we embraced, a feeling of warmth had once again returned to me. "Quick Ted, we have to go," and with that proclamation, we were getting back on the train she had just exited just seconds ago.

"Marilyn, Ted came to my room this morning," Marilyn's eyes couldn't help but perk up as I described my morning. "He asked how I was doing, and offered me something." While I revealed details to

Marilyn, my fingers once again met the vial I had in my possession in my pocket.

"He said that heaven is mine if I want it, as long as I give him something in return." Her eyes met mine, and could sense what was coming.

"Don't do it Ted, it isn't worth it!" she spoke before I revealed anything. "He shouldn't be trusted, and anything he offers should never be taken! You need to steer clear of him; how did you meet up anyway?" and as she asked the question, I realized how I had let him in.

"He disguised himself as you Marilyn, and I opened my door without hesitation." Without a word, she` simply wrapped around my arm and put her head on my shoulder.

The rest of the train ride over and the walk to the theater, I had her head resting on my shoulder. We could find comfort in each other, as stability in our current situations had become fragile. As we entered the theater, there wasn't a single empty seat and both The Circle and The Hope sat on stage. As we made our way down to our seats, I felt like every pair of eyes in the place was on us, except a very dark, soulless set that was dead ahead.

My mother gave me a confident look, and waved at me. As I waved back, I found Marilyn waving back at her as well. *Was she even waving at me?* I chuckled at my awkwardness, and blew her a kiss on stage. I wanted my mother to know I was staying strong, even though mentally, physically and emotionally I was completely drained.

Where is Mary Ann? Ted said she was attending this trial, and I have yet to see her. I need to see her and I want to see her! As my mind wandered, a man entered the stage. It didn't take me very long to realize who was walking towards the middle of the stage, as I had just spent a whole evening in Hell with him. Michael scanned the room, and met eyes with all The Hope, The Circle, and myself.

"Hello, and welcome back to the trial of Ted Wall. Today the topic under review is Greed. It should be stated that needs should trump the wants in lives, and overconsumption of wants lead to sin."

"The Hope will begin," he declared as he put his head down and walked back off stage. The screen began its slow dissension and once again my life had filled the room.

15

"You should really go home Ted, this work you have to do isn't going anywhere," my co-worker Bryce said as he tapped me on my shoulder. I looked at the clock and realized it was almost eight. "You have a girl at home waiting for you, and a girl like that shouldn't be kept waiting." He threw up his hand with a faint gesture of farewell, and the door closed behind him.

Sales jobs require patience, but also a lot of time. This job had started to take so much time, that the window I made myself available to Mary Ann was waning down to about two hours every night. We had been dating for about three years, but after I took this job six months ago my social time was at an all-time low. Mary Ann never said anything about it, because time spent equaled money in the bank. As our relationship moved forward, the natural things started to come up in conversation; everything from buying our own house to having kids. Our conversations as a couple were on a whole different level than what I was used to, but I found solace in my drive home.

As I got in my car, the forty-foot walk to my car left me drenched as the fall rain poured down, and I took a deep breath and turned on my car. The radio blared at me as I had not turned it down upon exiting, and the classic rock station began to ease my tired soul with the beautiful melodies of Eric Clapton reverberated around my car. The drive home gave me time to reflect on my current job situation, and how sales can be a tough job to handle sometimes. My main goal was to out sell my co-workers and retain the yearly incentive that comes along with it, though it became closer and closer with every day that passed…the time away from Mary Ann started to wear on me.

"Hey honey, where have you been my whole life?" Mary Ann ran over to me, pajamas donned her half-awake self.

"Another day, another dollar." Leave it to me for a four-word cliché to meet my beautiful partner, but the energy I had only left at the end of a workday permitted only weak statements.

"Ted, I know it is late, but I wanted to ask you something. Come into the kitchen with me; I already poured us some wine." She didn't waste any time diving into her thoughts, but as I followed her and she threw her arms up in a yawn that could rival any, I realized that I would do anything for this girl. *She is perfect, even when she is in pajamas lounging on the couch at home.*

"I got a call from a hospital at a small town outside of Cleveland. My mom threw out that I was looking for a full-time RN position, and they offered it to me on the spot today, over the phone. My mom is a good friend with the doctor that heads the department, so that aided in the decision, but as jobs go in my field, this ranks as a once-in-a-lifetime type deal," she took a sip of wine, and her eyes were fixated on me, waiting for the first words out of my mouth.

"Mary Ann, that is fantastic, I am so happy for you!" She glanced back at me with an uneasy sense.

"Ted, you know what that means though, you would have to vacate the job you just started, and uproot what we have laid down here." I knew that already, but hearing it from her gave me the understanding she truly cared about my situation as much as hers.

"That's fine, let me just finish out the year, cash out that bonus and we can go." She sipped her wine, and her eyes looked downward.

"Ted, I have to start as soon as possible. Jobs like this don't wait, they need to be filled." I took a deep breath, and pondered the moment. The idea of leaving the bonus on the table that I had been working so hard for hurt, and a middle ground seemed to be the only course of action.

"Mary Ann, let me stay. You go and stay with your mom. I will finish the year, and when I cash out I will give notice and be full time with you there, I promise." She walked over to me as I pleaded, and she put her arms around me.

"You promise this is okay? I know this job has been tearing you apart, and you know this job for me is life changing; for both of us." She looked at me, sinking her chin into my chest.

"Yes, I do, and I want you to take it. It's only two months we must sacrifice, for a jump start on the rest of our life." I kissed her forehead, and pulled her in close.

"Here so early Ted, did you even go home at all?" Bryce walked in with two cups of coffee, and as he passed my desk I realized he had both for himself, and didn't drop one on my desk.

"I didn't sleep too well. Mary Ann accepted a job near Cleveland. The idea of a long-distance relationship had settled in, and it is kind of weighing on me a bit." Bryce gave me a concerned look.

"Something that heavy seems like a decision that faces married couples, you two still feel like a high school fling, I mean that with no offense, sometimes I wish my wife and I still had that young love feel, but I didn't know the conversation on a Tuesday night was going to be so life changing." He sipped his coffee, and looked back at me with both eyebrows raised.

"Mary Ann is mature for her age, and our relationship will survive this. I have no doubts, and I am not going to leave before our year ends." Bryce fist pumped back at me, and shot me a wink, which reaffirmed my decision had that right financial path.

"Mary Ann, I miss you. I miss you with every single ounce of my body and soul, and I hope we are never apart like this again." Even though we had tried to see each other more, we only were able to squeeze in one visit in two months.

"Ted, I am proud of you! You stuck with your job and you are twenty-four hours away from a bonus, fifteen days away from a moving truck being parked in the driveway." The feeling of being with her again pulled at every inch of my body, and the phone sat silent for what felt like forever.

"I want you Mary Ann, I want and need you, and you will be seeing me soon, I will keep you up to date on the move."

The bank next to the house didn't close until seven on Fridays, and the day I got my bonus cut I made it to the bank at six fifty. The woman behind the desk seemed to sigh when she saw another customer sneaking in before close. I put my endorsed check on the counter, and told her I simply wanted to cash it.

"Mr. Wall, you do not want to deposit this?" she looked at the total of the check, and I simply just smiled and nodded my head, and she disappeared. She and her manager took a couple minutes to process the check, and soon bills were filling the counter. *Two months of my life for this*! I had to laugh at myself as I walked out of the bank with a small bulge in my pants, and made my way home. I barely slept that night, partially due to my plans the next day and the fact I had thousands of dollars tucked under my pillow, but as I did drift away, I felt proud that I was able to stick it out.

I pulled into the driveway of my new house, and the windows showed no sign of anyone being home. I rented a spot for the moving truck to sit overnight, as the three-hour drive down from Columbus had worn me out. Even though I was excited to be here, I did not want to look at boxes for at least the night. I put the fresh key in the keyhole, and was excited by the unfamiliarity of my surroundings. The smell of Mary Ann radiated around the bottom level of the house, and I found myself just lying on the couch and taking deep breath after deep breath. As my eyes remained closed, I could sense the soft glow of headlights in the driveway, and I perked up and waited for the door to open. There, after a ten-hour shift, was Mary Ann, entering the door, and quickly racing to the kitchen before she dropped all the groceries that weighted down her arms. I met her in the kitchen, picked her up and twirled around with her in my arms, and just held on to the embrace for as long as I could. She hadn't even said anything yet, and I felt like we hadn't been away from each other for more than one hour. Just as she regained composure and was looking for words, I cut her off.

"Mary Ann, I never want to be apart from you ever again," and as I got down on one knee, we never were.

The lights in the theater came back on, and I felt a collection of tears falling along with mine. The Hope's presentation had a way of filling me with optimism that was truly indescribable, as if re-living some of these moments a second time felt close to the emotion that came along with living it for the first time. Marilyn leaned over to me, and with watery eyes just gave me a hug from behind. *I love love.* Her words and ideas radiated through me with her touch, and I closed my eyes and let the moment hang on for a little while longer, as I knew what was coming. As I regained composure, the screen in the middle of the room slowly came down again, and the countdown made its way once again.

"It has to be a surprise Ted! We have gone through so much trouble to make this happen," my friend Reed barked at me, as I sat in the back of a car with a blindfold on, only being able to catch a glance of the feet of Mike and Evan, sitting on each side of me.

"Can't believe Ted is the last one of us to get married. I mean Casey over here already has two kids and Ted is just getting hitched, amazing," as Reed rambled on, I did realize that Mary Ann and I had taken our time, which was fine by me.

"Ted, do me a favor, for the next thirty-six hours, just go with the flow. This may be the last time we all have the ability to celebrate your pressing freedom of bachelorhood, and we all could use this time to let go a little bit." Reed got married the youngest of any of us, and with his admittance, it settled in where I may be going.

As my blindfold came off, the other four guys were already out of the car grabbing their luggage, and I was left by myself in the back of the car with a roundtrip ticket to Las Vegas staring back at me. As I examined the ticket, it was only for one day and night, but that seemed like just the right amount of time to appease my friends but to also be back in loving arms soon enough. As Reed and Evan hit on the stewardess, Mike and I tried to make a little bit of a plan of what we were going to do. We tried to remain secretive, because we knew the other three just had a couple things on their mind, and none of it was necessarily the best things. I felt a tap on my shoulder and as I looked back, a miniature bottle of vodka was staring back at me, and a toast was made. We were only forty-five minutes into our flight when the inhibitions of Ohio started to slowly leave all of us.

It really amazed me about how alcohol seemed to find its way into every facet of Las Vegas, and as we rode in a limo over to our hotel I was truly feeling no pain. At some point in our journey, every guy I was traveling with put his arm around me and told me something about their married life. Their confessions made me want to drink more and more, as I am assuming that's what the end goal was. We luckily received a quick check-in, dropped off our bags quickly, and before we knew it we were taking in the brisk fall air of the Las Vegas strip. The walk was quickly lubricated with frozen margaritas and we soon found ourselves at an Irish bar that had a live band rocking music you could hear from a good distance away.

As we entered, the ability to communicate became completely non-verbal, as Reed waved to the bartender who acknowledged his presence, and hopped out from behind the bar to embrace him. Reed had gone to college in Las Vegas; *I never understood that idea, a college in Las Vegas.*

Reed pointed at me, and the bartender threw me thumbs up and hopped behind the bar and poured a line of shots. As I approached the bar I grabbed a couple and started handing them out.

"No, no!" The bartender had to yell to get my attention, as my confusion settled in onto why he was shouting at me. "All of them are yours, on the house!" *This guy just poured me five shots, and wants me to shoot them all right now.* I felt an unbearable amount of peer pressure around me, and behind my four friends was a mini crowd that had begun to gather to observe the onslaught of intoxicating liquid. As I began shooting them, the different alcohols began to rage war on each other in my mouth, throat and stomach. Whiskey followed vodka, tequila followed whiskey, and even though the whole crowd of people behind me cheered me on and basked in my completion, the night slowly began to blur.

I found myself in the back of another limo, and as I examined my surroundings there were now more people with our group, both male and female. We were dropped off at a station casino, as Reed led the way exclaiming that this was his "old stomping grounds."

I found myself at a craps table, and as my cash became chips, the dice began to blur. I had a hard time processing exactly what was going on around me, but I did keep a watchful eye on the red, green and blue hiding underneath my hands. As the dice went around the table, the dealer pushed five die my way, and I picked two of them. *I am going to win myself a lot of money.* I wasn't a huge gambler, but I loved being in control. Even though my understanding of the game was that of a novice, I had been doing okay so far. As my die hit the back wall, I saw one of the dealers grab the money from the pass line. They pushed the die back to me, and tapped the table requesting more money be put down. Chips hit the table, and as the die hit the back wall, money was again taken off the line. After four rolls, people began leaving the table, leaving just Mike and I, and as he pulled his money from the table, he just simply stated that the table had gone cold, and walked away.

As the night was young, I snuck away to an ATM and retrieved more money, and slot hopped around the large bank of slot machines. As the slots ate my money, another ATM receipt was crumpled up and put in my back pocket, and again I found myself searching for the gambling holy grail on the roulette table, and it finally showed itself to me. I played numbers of significance, and as two of them hit in a row I finally saw myself with a decent amount of money in front of me. Sensing the numbers that were going to come, I began to press. The higher I got as the ball rotated around the wheel, the harder the fall came as my numbers didn't hit.

As the ATM once again spit me out money, Mike came and got me and explained a hasty change of scenery. The cold night air hit my face again, and as the limo retrieved all of us, the faces had once again changed, and as I processed them my mind went blank.

I came to as we came to an abrupt stop, and I felt a hand slap my knee, and Reed's smiling face looked back at me as he led me into a strip club. *So, fancy, even has a full restaurant and a full bar.* My mind started to wander as my body started to fantasize pleasures of both edible and visual sorts. As a cocktail was placed in my hand, my mind came to the realization that this was going to be the last thing I saw that night, and the last thing I drank that night.

As a girl walked out onto the stage, a different one walked over to me and whispered in my ear. She had found out I was the bachelor of the bachelor party, and she wanted me to come with her. I did not protest, as my vocal chords had been paralyzed by the power of Johnnie Walker. As we turned the corner we slipped into a room, and the song changed over the loud speaker.

The blonde woman came over and straddled my hips, and as her hips and body moved, the experience became out of body. My eyes took in the sights of a female body other than Mary Ann's, and my heart raced the whole time. I couldn't help but enjoy it, and while it was happening deep down I didn't want it to stop. I slipped my hand in my pocket and pulled out the leftover money I retrieved earlier, and I simply flashed it in her direction, and as she took it out of my hand, she leaned over and whispered softly to me "I am all yours."

My eyes seemed to take a while to retrieve my presence on the planet as I awoke, and I found myself uncomfortably close to Mike and Casey in a large bed. As I raised my head, it felt like someone bashed my head against the ground, and my eyes had a hard time registering anything past the pain.

"Morning Ted, what a night," Reed was brushing his teeth, and shaking all the others in the room. "Flight is in an hour and a half, we have to hurry!" Everyone groaned and the overall feeling of anger and supreme exhaustion filled the room. I drug myself around for the next hour, and soon found myself staring at my cell phone screen at the gate. Before the flight, I was able to uncover a couple of things from the night before, and as each one was slowly brought back to life, the worse I felt. The stripper's name was Patricia, and her number was saved uncomfortably close to my mother's. The photos I retrieved on my phone needed to be deleted, as some of them could come back to haunt me down the line, and most of them I did not remember. As I opened my banking application, the worst reality from the trip set in. My whole honeymoon fund was gone, and all I had to show for it was four crumpled up ATM receipts.

As the lights came back it was the first time I could remember during this whole process where I felt a weight in the room, and thousands of eyes on me. I didn't want to turn back and look, but I felt a familiar hand on my shoulder. When I turned back and looked at Marilyn, I was surprised to see her giggling and pointing at me, and I returned the laugh.

"It was a bachelor party," protesting my point, and looked back at the four men who made up The Circle and thought about how that memory of my life shouldn't have been shared. Especially by four other men, even if they are the leaders of hell, there has to be some sort of guy code everyone should follow, dead or alive. I looked over at the other side of the stage and The Hope were talking amongst each other, but as I caught my mother's eye I could see a slight smirk on her face too. *Everyone is laughing at me; great.* I returned the smile and made sure I held the eye contact as long as I could, for Michael was walking across the stage and calming the whole room down once again.

"Thank you, after review of the supreme sin of greed, we hereby find Ted Wall innocent, and grant him one night in heaven." As his words sang to my ears, I smiled, made eye contact again with my mother again, and as the world around me faded to white, I saw her mouth out three simple words. *"I love you."*

16

I awoke to find myself lying completely flat on my back looking to the sky. Huge cloud formations danced above me, and as I regained my senses I found myself on the outside of what looked like a palace. There were large columns that stood tall and as I slowly crept past them every wall and every hall I could see remained fully illuminated. I put my hand out and dragged it along the wall as I walked by, to my knowledge it looked and felt like marble, and there was not a single blemish that I could find.

As I continued, I found myself in a huge, open room that had no furniture and no windows, only a long staircase that raised itself before me, and I began to climb. As I walked up I felt the air around me thin a bit, and could feel my skin tense a bit at the sudden change in temperature. As I made it to the top, I looked back and did a quick estimate in my head of probably over three hundred stairs, and made my way slowly forward. Everything remained illuminated, but I could see the outside again as some areas were void of walls and ceilings.

I began to see the clouds hovering right above me. I soon walked out onto what felt like a back patio of sorts, except the fact that as far as my eyes could see was a marble floor, cloud formations at differing heights, and blue sky. *Heaven, this is what everyone imagines.* My mind raced with the ideas and thoughts of millions of below living on earth, and how this imagery seemed to fit right in with their beliefs. Just as I could fully assess my surroundings, a figure appeared behind me. "Well, Ted, finally we get to meet."

He couldn't have been more than six feet tall, with a slim figure. His hair was speckled with white and grey, and his full beard looked as though it fit him like a glove. My heart raced, and I began to examine and analyze the next moments in my mind. As our eyes met, the feeling in my body was something I had never felt before, and as I tested my senses everything felt alive and aware, yet numb to the moment.

"Who are you?" I had a knack for asking horrible questions at the perfect times. He laughed and approached me, and he put one his arms around me.

"Ted, all around the world people call me a lot of different things, but how about for now you come with me, we have a lot to see."

As he led me down a walkway, on both sides I started to feel a draft, and soon we were walking on a long narrow platform. There was blue sky and clouds surrounding us. My fear of heights crept in as I couldn't fully assess what was below, but I kept my eyes forward and followed. The silent walk covered about one hundred feet, and soon we came to the end of the platform, with nothing but blue sky below.

"Ted, my friend, in your experience here I need to show you something. It is something you have experienced yourself, as well as millions of others, to this day. One of my abilities, being what some people call 'The Almighty' is the ability to transfer the energy of souls as I see fit. Evelyn told you souls have the ability to live on, but tonight my friend, I am going to show you why." He spoke with such a presence I wanted to applaud and cry at the same time, but simply took his outreached hand in mine, and before I could grasp the situation as a whole, we were outside of a tall building, and he signaled me to follow behind him.

As we made our way back into the building and down the hallway, I sensed we were in a laboratory of some kind, and since it was after hours there wasn't a soul to be seen. Yet as we made our way down to the end of the hallway, we found a light shining out, and we crept into the room without making a single sound. We stopped, and began to examine what was going on in front of us. Although we were located within a couple of feet away from the gentleman looking into a microscope in front of us, it became clear that he was not aware of our presence at all.

"What is he doing?" again my question seemed so simple, but my level of intrigue was high.

"His name is Dr. Bradford Stills, and what he is looking into is the reaction of cannabis oil and cancer cells, as a form of treatment." As we looked on, my mind was trying to wrap around the whole situation I was in.

"See, Ted, I have sent souls from several deceased bright minds and inventors from years past and I have infused them with Dr. Stills here, raising his knowledge and sense of awareness, to try to assist in the aid of this generation of mankind. The souls that were passed on I refer to as 'service souls', just simply being souls that didn't get to complete their life's work in one life, so I have let them help another." As he finished speaking, Dr. Stills slammed his notebook down and threw his glasses across the room. He stared through us, sitting silent, but angry. "He will figure it out, I have faith in him," and as he said that, he exited the room and I had to run to keep up.

Again, we left the building. The night air hit my skin and I took in a deep breath. *Mother Nature at her best.* We made our way down the street a bit, and slowly entered the backside of a church. As we made our way inside he passed patrons that were silent on their knees, and went up to every single one and put his hands on their shoulders, muttered something under his breath, and moved along. The spiritual enlightenment in the room raised to a height I had never sensed before, and what I witnessed truly was unbelievable. There must have been twenty or so patrons that were blessed as we made our way down a set of stairs, and into a small classroom where a teacher sat with about nine or ten elementary aged children, listening as the teacher read a story back to them. We leaned up against the wall in the back, and listened in on the story, as the climax and resolution surged through the room. After the book was completed, the teacher and the children joined hands and bowed their heads in unison, and recited a calm prayer. I looked beside me, and he couldn't help but look back at me and smile.

As the children gathered their things, the parents started to trickle in and one by one and left in tandem until there was one left. The little boy sat patiently as the teacher joined him by his side. As the room became quiet there was a man entering the room, suit still proper as he had just come from work, and he smiled and embraced the boy with a joyful hug. As the father and the teacher exchanged greetings and thanks, I heard a soft proclamation.

"Sometimes it is hard for a family to move on without the mother, but sometimes the love that was lost can be found in a different form. I do not have the power to reincarnate someone that is deceased, but their soul can be found in another body to promote love and the well being of the fallen. I call these 'secondary souls', and around the world these are the most prevalent, as when they pass all they search for is the love of the ones they left behind."

We exited the classroom and made our way back out to the street with haste, with the slow hue of daylight creeping onto the horizon. We made our way down the street and eventually made our way to a neighborhood, and crept into a dark two-story house, and made our way up the stairs. As we made the turn into what looked like the master bedroom, we were confronted with a woman kneeling bedside, crying, as her hands remained interlocked towards the ceiling.

"God, it's me, Meredith, and I want you to know I am very upset with you. Why did you have to take him? Why did it have to happen to me?" Her crying continued as her head rested on the edge of the bed, and we watched on in silence.

"Some souls never get to me Ted, and I cannot release them back or let them embrace the afterlife. I call these 'lost souls', and although sadness and anger usually are a byproduct, there is unfortunately nothing that I or anyone else can do." As he spoke of them, he put his hand on my shoulder and we were once again walking down the long, narrow platform from before. He turned, and looked at me with a smile on his face.

"Ted, you have a beautiful soul and peacefulness about you, and I hope you know as the process goes on to decide your fate, I am on your side. I wanted you to see tonight and process it, for every interaction the living has on earth is one that should be treated equally, and cherished. There isn't a clear-cut system of rules and regulations to follow when it comes to the dead interacting with the living, but the main purpose is just to achieve a sense of tranquility on both sides. Although some may find peace, some may be left searching for it their whole lives. I wish you luck Ted, and remember one thing, when one life ends, another begins." As he finished speaking the sun hit the horizon. The sunlight drowned out my surroundings and I once again found myself lying on my bed, with a heavy heart, and a sense of peace that I had never felt before.

17

I got up out of bed with a spring in my step I hadn't felt in a while, and shuffled over to the collection of music sitting next to my record player. I fingered through a couple albums and slowly slid one out, and laid it down. Coldplay was always a favorite of mine, as I always found solace in their music. I made my way to the bathroom, and tried to clean myself up the best I could. As I shuffled over the closet I heard a knock on the door, and this time I was reluctant at first because Ted was the last person I wanted to see. I opened the door an inch and peered out, and a smiling face looked back at me.

"Come on now, open it, it's me!" Marilyn pushed the door away to enter as she grazed me and began a little dance as Chris Martin sang on. She lay back on the bed and threw her arms back, and my mind realized at that moment how I felt inside is how Marilyn acted on the outside.

I opened my closet and examined what I had at my disposal and just as I reached out there was a hand shooting past mine into the closet.

"Wear this one, it matches my outfit perfectly!" She held up a bright pink tie against her bright pink dress, and I offered no resistance. I walked over and stood by the mirror, and threw the tie around my neck.

"I never have fully understood ties, I mean does dressing up really have to come with being mildly strangled all day?" I heard a faint laugh from the bed as I completed my beauty noose.

"Ties were probably created by the same person who created high heels." I couldn't help but laugh as Marilyn took off her high heel and proceeded to show me how tall and uncomfortable they were. I walked over towards the door and as I reached out for the handle, I felt two arms around my chest. As she hugged me she put her head on my back. "I am proud of you; you are doing well." I closed my eyes and took her words in, and without any more words exchanged we left the room.

As we made our way outside, the smell of cotton candy filled the air. White and red roses all around us created a beautiful hue of pink that danced in the air, and in the moment walking over to the station, I was on quite a high. As we approached the train, I once again examined the 'TRS' on the top, as it became an all too familiar sight. Marilyn shuffled over to the window, and once again we were off.

"Marilyn, I have to tell you about last night," I said as she looked back at me with intrigue. "The idea of souls living on got taken a step further, as I spent all night being shown all the different ways souls can be reborn again, to help and to love." Marilyn just sat and smiled as I rambled. "You know Marilyn, if I end up being awarded Heaven in the end, I may volunteer to return. The idea of helping is so noble, and I would love to make that commitment." Marilyn wrapped around my arm and smiled.

"Does every soul get the chance?" Her words hovered a bit, and I found myself feeling the first bit of nervousness in my stomach.

"Some souls never do get the chance, the ones who don't make it." She didn't reply to me, she just grasped my arm tighter as the train roared on.

As the train slowed and approached again, my heart raced. It wasn't easy to come down off the high heaven gives you. As we walked in, it once again remained quiet, and the receptionist waved us through. We continued to make the trek down the hallway, when suddenly Marilyn grabbed me and swung a door open and began to race upwards.

"What are you doing?" She didn't reply as she just began to climb upwards. *Stairs.* My legs burned with protest as I went two at a time. We reached a set of double doors and Marilyn snuck through them without making much of a sound.

As we entered we were greeted with a long, beautiful bar covering the whole room. The bar and the room itself were littered with patrons here to observe, and as they saw us enter they began to crowd around us. Every single person went on to hug both Marilyn and I, throwing back cheers of support. A tall gentleman came over and bear hugged me, lifting me off the ground a little bit.

"We are rooting for you guys, we have faith in you both." He dropped me back and gave the same hug and pep talk to Marilyn. *Rooting for us.* I appreciated all the unconditional love that I was getting; it seemed to be the perfect distraction before the trial resumed. Marilyn met eyes with me, and pointed her head at the bar.

"Whiskey, straight." Marilyn's demands caught the bartender off guard a bit, but she winked at him and he melted on command. She raised one of the glasses, "To you!" She toasted my glass, threw the alcohol back and headed for the door. As the whiskey burned its way down my throat I took the stairs one by one, as Marilyn giggled in front of me.

We entered the theater and made our way down, and once again found our seats. My waning high of heaven was soon over taken by a faint numbness from the whiskey, and I smiled and sat back. As the eight familiar faces began to make their way on stage, Ted veered off into the middle of the stage. He waited for the room to become silent and still, and began to speak.

"Welcome back to the trial of Ted Wall. Our topic of discussion today is Gluttony. Seems like overindulgence and overconsumption has become a norm with some these days, but it should never be that way. To consume more than one needs and to keep it out of the hands of others is one of the worst practices, and gluttony will remain one of the worst sins one can commit. The Hope, you may begin." As Ted finished the whole room went quiet, amazed how one man can suck the life and air out of a room. No set of eyes met mine. All faced forward as the screen dropped yet again.

18

I stood there, my palms sweating and my mouth uncomfortably dry, just staring down the aisle. The silent energy radiated around me, and as I looked back at Mike, he just kept his hands in front of him and winked back at me. *I wish my mom were here; she would have loved to be here.* When Mary Ann had asked me what song she should walk down the aisle to, I told her to surprise me. So, as I stood here, the silence lingered and I didn't know what was coming next. My heart warmed as Matt Simons serenaded the room, a favorite of hers. She smiled as she appeared, and everyone rose. She didn't let me look at the dress before she stood in front of me, and it looked amazing. The next nine minutes of my life will be forever remembered as the best in memory, and the night that ensured is a close second.

Mary Ann and I walked in to the banquet room, and the eighty-people staring at us rose and applauded, as Mike walked up and handed us both glasses of champagne. After reciting words and a singular kiss, the champagne quenched my thirst and gave me new life, as I made my way to a table with two chairs. A speech from Mike, a speech from the maid of honor, and a couple of words from yours truly to ease the crowd and unveil the beautiful three course meal. I sat down and couldn't help but choke up, because as I addressed the crowd the thought of my mother clouded my thinking, but as the night went on, the sadness I felt was drowned with bubbly and pre-made cocktails. Three courses slowly made their way, as family members and friends came up to the table and exchanged congratulations and took photos.

Mary Ann and I smiled at each other as we graced the dance floor by ourselves, and Steven Tyler created tears all around the room. When the song was over, Mary Ann continued to dance with her grandfather, and I made my way over to the bar.

"Whiskey, neat." I developed a love for whiskey in college. Being from Ohio I kind of just found Kentucky bourbon a must. The deep amber color, the smoky vanilla flavors from the wood, and the burn as it went down. The day had started completely stone cold sober, and now that was a distant memory. I took off Mary Ann's garter and threw it into a sea of single men, and she returned the favor throwing her flowers into a sea of single women. After we returned to our seats, we sat and watched as the music kept our crowd moving, and embraced each other as husband and wife.

"Let's get the happy couple over here!" Our DJ stopped the music and guided us over to the cake, and I laughed at Mary Ann as we stood by a five-tier cake that could feed an army. She chuckled at me as I examined the cake, slowly cut into it, grabbed a piece, and fed it to her bite by bite. With every bite, I stared into her beautiful green eyes, and the crowd applauded as she took in the carrot-flavored delight. I put the knife down, and Mary Ann took it in her hand and waved it at the spectators, looking for more applause as she began to cut. The piece she cut could barely fit on the pale white plate and she put the knife down. She grabbed the piece and time stood still as the cake came flying into my face. I could feel icing in every nook and cranny of my face, and the laughter that ensued filled the room. I couldn't help but smile at her aggressive cake tactics, as I was able to finally fork feed myself some to try after the derail was complete.

A representative from the hotel walked over to Mary Ann and I and whispered the idea of curfew, and we laughed a bit when we realized it was way beyond our originally scheduled time to have the whole night complete. Mary Ann and I stumbled over to the DJ and grabbed the microphone, and gave a general last call statement. The remaining people who continued gyration to the hits made their way over to the bar and topped off their night with all forms of inhibition prohibiting liquid.

Mary Ann and I were the last ones in the room as the cleaning crew came in and congratulated us. I grabbed the half full bottle of champagne from our table and walked up to our room with my arm around Mary Ann. As we entered I took a swig and handed it over to her as she unzipped her dress, took a swig from it and walked over to the IPod dock and thumbed through the music selection. As she walked over to me, she passed the bottle of champagne over to me, and lay back on the bed. The last full memory created that night was that of me making my way back over to the bed, with Tove Lo filling the room.

As the lights came back on in the theater, I just stared over in my Mother's direction, and caught a glimpse of the tears streaming down her face. Although I had asked the question a million times in my head, I still didn't know why I had to lose my mother so young, and for her to see the wedding day up close and personal meant so much to me. While rest of The Hope consoled her, she looked back at me with tear filled eyes, and I couldn't help but throw up a faint wave with tears now streaming down my face. Two familiar arms closed in around me, and I could hear a soft sob coming from behind me as I looked back.

"The idea of love can only be matched by that of true love, and for it to be witnessed by the ones you love is one of the greatest things one can have," Marilyn's words stuck to me, and the warmth I felt from her soothed the burn. Ted was walking across the stage, and as he raised his hand the whole theater went completely silent, and he smiled as he walked back to his chair with one finger raised up to his lips. I gathered myself, and my heart raced at the idea of The Circle's rebuttal, and the faint imagery of Ted smiling lingered in my mind as the room went dark again.

"Ted, my family expects us in twenty minutes, we have to go!" I grabbed the keys off the table and raced to the car. "Now remember, my brother will be there. He just got out of a relationship and is kind of on edge, so just keep the opinions to a minimum," she spoke like a drill sergeant. "My parents are both remarried and they have agreed to remain civil today, as this will be the first Thanksgiving they will be seated at the same table, all four of them." She continued to race down the mental list of our first full holiday meal together and continued.

"My cousin Melissa is kind of a handful. She and her husband are complete recluses, and when they come out and get a little bit of alcohol in them their opinions seem to flow a little bit easier than normal." I nodded my head. Before she could continue, I put my hand up and silenced her.

"Mary Ann honey, please. Everything will be okay, just relax." She looked back and me and took a deep breath.

"Did you remember the wine?" As her words left her mouth, my foot hit the brake. *Dammit.*

As we entered the house, conversation flooded the room. Multiple people embraced us, and the onslaught of congratulations continued, as our wedding was only a couple of week's prior. I made my way to the kitchen to a brief silence, and found myself alone with multiple cabernets looking back at me. I poured myself a glass and slowly drank my way out of uneasy conversation, and took in the blood of life.

"You found yourself the dinner stash, did you?" Mary Ann's father was an intimidating figure, standing a good six inches taller than me with arms that seemed to barely be contained within his shirt. "Come on, let me introduce you to something a little bit stronger before dinner." He lead me upstairs to a room with dark leather furniture, and bookcases and one large window facing the backyard. "This is called Jefferson Ocean, a specialty bourbon. Go on, give it a try." He handed me a glass that stood about halfway full, and in that moment, I obliged half out of fear and half out of the need to ease the night.

"I am happy for you and Mary Ann, you seem happy." His eyes never left mine as he spoke, and I nodded back to him.

"Never been happier in my life, sir." As I spoke he laughed a bit, and poured us both another half a glass.

"Ted, I have been married twice. In the moment, your world seems so one dimensional, all about her, nothing else matters. Just remember, take care of yourself too, never lose sight of what's the best for both of you," he said as he clanked my glass and took another strong swig. I mirrored him, realizing my empty stomach could use some backup to the onslaught of alcohol in the last thirty minutes. "Come on, the wolves are waiting," he chuckled. He made his way back downstairs, as I followed closely behind him. I walked over to Mary Ann and gave her a kiss on her cheek. The strong liquor smell made her recoil, and she gave me a side eyed glanced that meant business.

Prayers were said, plates got passed, and the dinner seemed to start to blur together. There was no shortage of red wine as I continued to enjoy multiple glasses, to the mild protest of my wife. As Mary Ann's dad threw out inappropriate jokes and lewd comments towards other people, I couldn't help but laugh at his pure lack of political correctness at the table.

"Let's raise a toast, to my ex-wife and new wife, for being so civil. To my son, for not crying over a picture of Cynthia at the table. To Melissa, for coming out of hibernation to eat a free meal and say hello to everyone." Mary Ann's dad swigged from his glass and laughed to himself. I swigged too, and nudged Mary Ann when she didn't raise her glass. She looked at me, threw her napkin down and left the table.

"Honey, what are you doing? What are you doing out here? The dinner is almost over." I had a hard time completing sentences as turkey and red wine battled in my stomach.

"Ted, you know, it is hard enough to be at the same table as this dysfunctional group, but when you get completely smashed it really just does not help." I could feel a wave of reality and soberness come over me, and I sat down next to her.

Mary Ann continued, "The reason why my mother left my father was alcohol. He never fully understood his problem, and now he is not only jabbing at her at a dinner table, he is infiltrating my marriage!" She cried harder as the realization flooded the scene. I put my arm around her, and searched for the correct words to console her. All I could muster was a faint "I love you," and a soft sob of my own. Mary Ann's mother made her way outside and stood over her, and whispered the plan of getting her out of the predicament she was in. As they embraced each other, I leaned in to hug them both. As I looked down, I closed my eyes. Suddenly, without notice, the battle that waged between the food and drink of the night came to a completion, as it made its way out of my mouth all over my mother in law.

As the lights came back on in the theater, the embarrassment I felt was amplified by the fact that whiskey was still digesting in my stomach, as I had to witness one of the most uncomfortable moments of my life. *Low blow.* The lights remained on, and as we waited for a verdict Marilyn grabbed me and motioned for me to leave the theater with her.

We retreated to the bar where we were before, and the whole room was empty. Marilyn hopped behind the bar and grabbed a bottle of whiskey and poured two glasses. She raised her glass, and handed me mine.

"To the past." She met my glass and shot hers back, and I followed suit. As the lights started to flicker, Marilyn ran over and locked the door and came over and embraced me.

"I can't handle anymore." She looked up at me with tears in her eyes, and I brought her in close.

"I'll be okay, we'll be okay." I proclaimed confidence in something I was not confident in at all, but in the moment, it needed to be said. I walked out onto the ledge and looked down at Ted on stage, as he addressed the crowd. I didn't hear the verdict but his eyes soon found mine, and as he raised his arms, the whole theater went completely dark. The only thing I could make out was a pair of eyes, blood red and illuminated staring back at me from the stage, and as the lights came back on there was not a single person anywhere to be seen. I retreated behind the bar, and soon heard a pull at the door. The struggle continued as the pulling and jarring became more violent. I grabbed the bottle of whiskey and put it straight to my mouth, and as the burn hit my throat the door flew across the room, and Ted stood at the entrance breathing deep and heavy. He walked over to the bar, and with one swift motion he grabbed the bottle from my hand and drained it dry. He put the bottle back down, took a step back with his hands outstretched on the bar, and as he exhaled a string of fire swallowed me whole.

19

My hands remained clenched and my jaw was locked from gritting my teeth so hard. Although the fire had done no physical damage, the heat that hit my flesh created the worst pain I have ever felt. As the feeling subsided, it felt like I was regaining skin all over my body, like I was molting a suit of fire. I tried to take in my surroundings, but all I could see was black on all sides, and a faint glow above me. As I extended my arms out and touched the walls around me, crumbs started to fall to my feet. I went in close and took a deep breath, *dirt.* I took a moment to stare straight up as the glow illuminated the sky, but my panic started to settle in when I realized I couldn't get a good footing or grasp anywhere where I was. *Trapped.* I sat back down on the ground and forced myself to take deep breaths as I contemplated the situation. *What was the verdict? Where is Ted? Where did everyone in the theater go?* The image of Ted spitting fire haunted my memories; I tried to not even blink because the momentary darkness brought his face back. Just as I calmed myself down, I felt a splash of something on my head. I reached up and ruffled my hair to get the foreign material out of it. I felt a brief crawl, and quickly disposed of it with a swift right hand. Again, a splash, and more dirt hit me bringing along with it the slow crawl of insects inside of it. The dirt became to come heavier from above, and as the fourth spill came in, extreme panic hit me.

It didn't take long for the dirt to reach my knees, making it harder for me to get around the small enclosure I found myself stuck in. When the dirt first started coming down it was one batch at a time, now there was no pause as dirt flew from all directions. I tried to use the dirt building up as a base to climb, but as I made a last-ditch effort to throw my hand up the hole I was in grew another three feet, and I fell back down in the dirt flat on my back. My breathing became sporadic as the dirt all around me moved slowly up and down my skin. When I sat up, my legs sank into the dirt. It was now about chest high, and final realizations were dawning on me. My legs became immobile, and my arms followed suit not too long after. My chin was raised up, and air was at a premium. Some of the dirt now entered my mouth, and despite my protest I began to slowly chew and swallow some. My head became submerged, and again I found myself losing one sense at a time, until all I could do was feel the crawling all around me and the grip of the dirt take hold.

Underneath my feet, I could feel a rumbling and my senses returned as I fell to a cold hard floor, and all four limbs were flailing as I tried to regain my sense of being and my sense of balance. I coughed up dirt violently and my fingers dug at my eyes, nose and ears finding dirt everywhere. As I came to, I heard laughter all around me, and my eyes scanned where the noise was coming from. Vlad, Adolf and Joseph stood about fifteen feet away, drink in hand laughing hysterically. Ted walked over to them and shooed them away. Above me suspended was a container, and it was suspended about twenty feet off the ground. *They watched it happen, and laughed.* Anger built up inside of me, but as I got to my feet and rushed in Ted's direction, he simply put out one hand and I became completely immobile.

"Follow me," as he put his hand down, my body became mobile again, and I stumbled as the loss and regaining of balance threw me off. I follow Ted down a long, black hallway only illuminated by the soft glow of torches on the wall, and although I tried to catch up I could never get relatively close to Ted at all.

As I kept up with him, he started descending stairs, and as a slight bout of vertigo came over me, there seemed to be thousands of stairs, and as I went down slowly one by one I could have sworn Ted was floating down them, and it was hard to even keep up. We finally reached the bottom after what felt like an hour, and two double doors swung open. Ted made his way to the other side of the room. I slowed my pace as I entered the room, looked around to see openings, and an illuminated glow filling the room. Ted sat behind a large oversized desk, black as night with claws on the bottom.

"Come!" He gestured for me to sit across from him, and although my body protested my legs moved without control. "Have you put any thought into my offer?" He stared at me directly, no hesitation in his voice.

"I…can't, I won't sacrifice her for myself." Ted smiled as I spoke, and anger filled my body again.

"That really is a shame. That was the last time I was going to offer." He stood up again and walked past me. "Come, I have something to show you," he said as he raised his hand and my body jolted up, and we were once again making our way down the black hallways as the fire blazed on both sides.

He opened a door and we slowly made our way down the left side of the hallway, while my mind started to recognize these areas. As Ted floated before me, I started to feel eyes on both sides of me. The condensation on the windows became dense with the heavy breathing of people staring out onto me, and as we passed dozens of rooms, I began to hear moaning and screaming fill the air. Ted stopped, turned around and stared back at me.

He extended out one finger and as he retracted it back to himself, my body flew through the air and within seconds I was a foot away from him. He put his hand on my shoulder. I recoiled as his fingers seared my skin with a pain like an open flame, and he pulled me in closer.

"Open the door Ted," he pointed out to the handle, and as I pushed the door open, my whole entire world came crashing down. *Mary Ann!*

I ran over and slid down to her, and her beautiful green eyes looked up at me, filled with tears. As I embraced her, her cold skin shocked my body. Only seconds passed and our embrace was cut short, as Ted slowly pulled me back. I pushed his hand off me and raced back towards her, but I soon felt my whole entire body seize, and I couldn't move or make a sound. Mary Ann stared back at me, and as our eyes were locked she couldn't make a sound. She sat back, and pulled her knees closer to her chest, and sank her head in. I screamed as loud as I could, but no sound came out. I felt a deep burn around my neck as Ted lifted me up, and threw me back into the hallway. The door closed, and I made my way back to the window, but my heavy breathing fogged my view.

My body was pulled back and despite a heavy protest, once again I was being moved against my will. The emotions thundering inside my body created a violent outburst with my arms thrashing around me, but Ted just laughed and continued back. We made our way back to the office, and I fell to my knees in front of him, as he stood behind his desk.

"Why, why is she here? Why are you doing this to her?" I wanted to cry, but the heat in the room dried my tears before they came.

"She is beyond saving Ted. She has been mine all along, and soon you will be too." As his words made their way to me, he raised his arms, and all the walls and furniture in the room fell away, and it was just fire scorching all around us. The fire crept in closer, and soon I was surrounded in it and there was no retreat possible. His tall figure glided through the flames, and he was standing over me. He reached out his finger and the burn was unbearable as he made two crossing lines over my heart. He threw his head back and laughed, and his foot came rushing towards my chest and I was thrown back into the fire with the force of his kick. As the heat trapped me, my world went black.

20

My body felt like it was still on fire as I awoke, but the tears running down my cheeks were as cold as ice. *He has her, and there isn't anything I can do.* There was a battle of sense waging in my head, and I couldn't find any of it. *I am one verdict away from going to hell.* My right arm began to numb, as my anxiety seemed to always affect me physically. I rubbed my arm up and down from shoulder to fingertip, and sat back on the bed.

"*She always has been.*" His voice rang through my head, and despite my best efforts, the idea that he had broken me was manifesting itself. I turned on the cold water in the shower, stood in it and let my whole body go numb while battling the want to shiver and cry.

Turning off the water, I wrapped a towel around my body and looked at myself in the mirror. I reached out my hand and touched my mirror, and then touched myself. *Is this real?* I walked over and tried to block the voices in my head with music, and the second I dropped the needle I heard a familiar knock on the door. Marilyn made her way into the room without a sound, and gave me a concerned look.

"Ted, what happened in the theater caused a pretty widespread panic, we didn't know if you would come back," she came up and hugged me, and her hands felt so warm against my cold skin.

"Marilyn, he has Mary Ann, and he showed me. I was in her cell! He wouldn't let me talk, and he wouldn't let me..." I trailed off again due to the dismay that swept through my body, and sat down on the couch.

"It's taking a toll on you, I can tell, and with you one verdict away..." Marilyn now trailed off as a very uncomfortable idea overcame her. I got up and walked over to the closet, and as I reached out for clothes, I motioned to Marilyn to turn around, and she simply put her hands over her eyes. I proceeded to put on a light blue tee shirt, and some jeans. I went over to the couch and sat down by her, and put on my tennis shoes.

"Marilyn, I am going today and requesting a recess from the trial. Mentally, emotionally and physically I don't know if I can handle much more of this, and if I am going to go back I need just a little bit of time to catch my breath." As I finished Marilyn closed her eyes, nodded and patted me on the knee. "Let me go change Ted, meet you downstairs in five."

I sat outside on the bench, and took slow breaths, and as my lungs filled, I exhaled slowly. As my lungs emptied, I could see and feel my heart beat in my chest, and I just simply smiled at the idea of time off. *I'll be back Mary Ann. I'll be back Mom.* I racked my brain for ideas to get word to them, but I settled on the fact that time off was needed, and it's a decision I must make for myself. I got up and paced back and forth, when I felt a hand on my shoulder from behind.

"Let's go," Marilyn had thrown on a pair of jeans as well with flats, and her blouse fluttered in the wind. She walked to the train with purpose, and she sat up against the window and stared off into the trees that swayed on the other side of the tracks. She looked back at me and smiled, as the train rushed forward.

When we arrived, Marilyn was again up and out before me, and she swung the doors open. As we made our way to the receptionist she gave me a look that screamed hope and relief, as the way I exited the theater the day before must have resonated through everyone here. I waved my hand, and made my way up behind Marilyn.

"Yes, what can I do for you?" she spoke so softly and peacefully.

"We would like to request a recess," Marilyn demanded. The receptionist spun around in her chair and looked through files and pulled out two pieces of paper. She presented me one with a pen and she presented another next to me with Marilyn's name on it. I took the pen and signed on the line and gave the paper back, and as I did Marilyn held the pen in her hand. I looked down and saw the same piece of paper, but as she signed the pen weaved its way through four other signatures on the paper.

"Hope to see you both soon." She went on to put the papers back in the files, and waved goodbye. With arms locked, Marilyn and I made our way back to the train. I shuffled over to the window and sat looking out, again taking deep breaths and calming myself. As the train began to slowly move again, and I saw my mother walk out to the end of the walkway. I put my hand up on the window, and she simply waved back at me with a smile on her face.

The train ride felt a lot quicker as it slowed again, and Marilyn once again rushed out, almost with hop in her step. As we got back out into the station, she grabbed me by both arms.

"Ted, we aren't going back. I have something to show you, you have to come with me!" She exuded a sense of confidence and longing that I couldn't turn down, and simply nodded my head to her. "Trust me Ted," as she pleaded, she walked back towards the tracks. She stood at the end of the platform, and as the train moved again I walked up behind her.

"Don't stand so close, I don't want you to fall." The train rushed past and the end made its way past us. The second the train was cleared, Marilyn jumped down into the void where the tracks were laid, "Come on!" she yelled at me as I stood above her watching as she climbed over the tracks. I jumped down, and the slight sting in my ankles threw me off balance. When I made my way over the large tracks, Marilyn was standing on the other side, and she requested I help boost her up on the other side. While she was able to surface quite easily, I had a hell of a time lifting myself up and the burn from my forearm's struggle made its way into my shoulders and my back. Before I could even rest as I surfaced on the other side of the tracks Marilyn was entering the trees and quickly was out of sight.

"Where are we going?" I yelled out, but Marilyn had picked up pace and the only thing I could see was her blonde hair in the distance. The trees all around were tall and thick, with foliage completely blocking any form of light that existed, so as I walked on footing was becoming difficult to maintain because of the darkness that made its way around me. If I had to estimate, I would say I covered about a mile on foot, and all I did was followed the giggles and the faint "Hurry!" echoing in front of me. I finally approached Marilyn as she had stopped, and she turned around and hugged me. I put my arms around her and closed my eyes, and as our embrace ended I could hear voices and see faint hints of light in the distance, and again Marilyn was making her way forward again.

We approached what looked like a village, with every building made of materials I would imagine they just found in this forest, and before I entered the opening I sat back and watched as Marilyn made her way into the crowd. She was embraced by a multitude of people as she entered, and yelled back at me. I entered the clearing and people began to make their ways to all sides of me, and I was being hugged and embraced by so many people.

"Hello, nice to meet you, how are you?" I couldn't keep up with all the introductions and questions and just simply nodded my head as the groups of people subsided. Marilyn came back to me and grabbed my hand, and we made our way to a large circular clearing with a large bon fire raging in the middle. The fire threw flames in the air with such a beautiful grace and elegance, and I was transfixed on it. Marilyn ushered me into a large hut with people sitting and standing all around, and she walked me over to what looked like a bar. Soon I had a very stout beverage in my hand, and the whole room became very quiet.

The other side of the hut had a singular chair on a raised platform, and applause thundered as a disheveled blonde haired man sat down with a guitar. I had to rub both eyes and squint a bit to fully confirm who was sitting in front of me, but as the first lines rang out, it was as real as it could be. The whole room seemed to melt away as Kurt Cobain sat alone on the chair, and his words suffocated the emotion in the room. Marilyn had made her way closer, and was sitting with her legs crossed on the ground, and I squeezed my way in and sat next to her. She put her finger up against her lips for me to remain quiet, and I nodded to her. As he sang on, his blue eyes scanned the room and met mine, and for a brief moment, his music had me under a spell.

The applause once again thundered around the room as he got up and bowed and made his way off the makeshift stage in front of us. Marilyn wiped her eyes and made her way back to the bar area.

"Marilyn, that was amazing, what is this place?" She smiled as I probed, but she simply patted my arm.

"I'll be back." She exited before I could interject again, and I was simply left alone at the bar. As I drank on, I watched as all different types of people interacting around me, and everyone seemed to be so happy. As my third drink was making its way down, my heart dropped at the sight I saw, and I couldn't help but gasp a little.

"Mark? Mark Torin?" I walked over and embraced him, and he pulled away a little until he recognized me. "What are you doing here? I haven't seen you since…" I trailed off at the thought of his letter in the newspaper.

"Hello Ted. It sure is nice to see you; isn't this place nice?" his eyes showed content, and my heart was overwhelmed thinking of his story on the news.

"Mark, so many people, the whole city was devastated," my thoughts became jumbled as he was once again in front of me.

"Ted, I regret it every single day, I just became a victim of circumstance, and looking back I don't know how I let it go so far," a tear formed in his eye as his recollection took place. I embraced him again, and felt the energy from a lost friend returned to me.

"How did you end up here?" I prodded when I felt able.

"I was de-briefed, and was given a room to live, well, you know," he smiled a little and continued. "They told me about a possible trial, and as the weeks and months went on a trial never came, so my curiosity built up and led to me wandering all over." My body felt heavy at his realization. "One day, I saw the train leave and someone appear from underneath the tracks. She climbed up and over the opposite side, and disappeared into the trees. I made my way to the other side, and here I am." His nonchalant demeanor was both refreshing and concerning, and before he could prod into my story Marilyn was once again by me, and she quickly introduced herself.

"Come on, you aren't going to want to miss this," Mark gave me a nod as I left with Marilyn, and was soon in a huddle of people by the bon fire.

"Do you think God gets stoned? I mean I sure do think so, look at the platypus!" Laughter filled the air. I realized the classic joke was coming from a master himself.

"Robin, tell the one about golf!" Marilyn giggled as Robin returned the laughter in kind.

"Oh, honey you mean where you can dress like a pimp and no one will care?" The whole crowd erupted in laughter as I felt a nudge from behind.

"Got a light?" said a rugged man with a cigarette standing with an outstretched hand. I shook my head and realized who was standing next to me.

"Mr. Hemingway, it truly is an honor to meet you." He smirked as I professed my love, and nodded.

"Wish it was under different circumstances; this guy seems funny though," he pointed toward Robin as he pulled out another cigarette and handed it to me. "Find a light for us," I walked around and finally was able to just light a twig on fire and light both cigarettes.

"These things will kill you!" Marilyn took the cigarette out of my hand and acted like she was going to throw it on the ground, but instead she took a drag and handed it back.

"Oh, hello Ernest, nice to see you." She walked over and gave him a hug, and he seemed truly happy in the embrace. "Like I said before, I'm sorry I ruined high school for you," Marilyn laughed and threw up a hand in carelessness as Ernest professed his sorrow, and my mind truly couldn't wrap itself around what I was witnessing.

Marilyn and I made our way to the outer edge of the village, and all the sounds of music, laughter and conversation serenaded the night sky.

"It's good to see you relaxed Ted; it's refreshing." Her smile illuminated my world, and in the moment, I was calm.

"Marilyn, you have been here before." She nodded and smiled, and looked the other way.

"I never thought I was going to leave, but circumstances changed, and I wouldn't have had it any other way," she grabbed my arm and pulled me away from the village. I wanted to prod more, but in the moment, I had no cares, and I was putting off taking on anymore. The path darkened as we made our way through the trees, and a faint crisp smell rose in the air. We made our way into a clearing, and in front of us stood large trees surrounding a small pond sitting still, looking like it had never been touched ever. As we made our way down to the edge of the pond, we heard a rush of air from beside us, and a loose vine hung in the air. The splash from the water reached our feet, and soon we saw a woman emerge from the water.

"Come on Heath, you told me we were going at the same time!" I looked behind me and saw Heath Ledger himself standing on a branch, vine in hand.

"Brittany, I wanted to see you do it first. I needed inspiration," I looked back and saw Brittany Murphy laughing and making her way back to the edge of the pond. Another rush of air stormed by, and this time the splash saturated both Marilyn and me.

As we proclaimed our displeasure of being wet, Brittany and Heath stared back at us.

"Um, excuse me, if you are going to be here there are a couple of rules," we stood at attention as Brittany yelled at us from the water. "First, you have to climb that tree and swing from the vine like we just did. Second, you have to lose the clothes." They both laughed and started swimming again, and Marilyn was beginning her ascent up the tree. *This is happening.* Despite my mental protest, I found myself steadying on a branch about twenty feet above the water. Marilyn looked out onto the water, and then back at me as one by one buttons loosened. As the top of her body became bare, my heart barely stayed in my chest. She leaned over and dropped her jeans, and soon I was seeing Marilyn in a way I never had before. *Well, besides in a magazine or two.* I heard muted screams of excitement and enjoyment from the water, but I couldn't take my eyes off her. Her ivory skin made their way through the air, and soon she was submerged underneath the water, and the cheers from the others became more pronounced.

"Come on Ted!" She swam in place, staring back up at me as my clothed body steadied on the branch. I reached down and began to pull my shirt over my head, and a mix of excitement and nervousness seized my arms above my head. Despite losing my clothes, my body began to become warmer. Once I was free from my pants, I took a moment to realize where I was, and how I was presenting myself to my three-person audience. Although there was no light present in the sky, there was a full moon tonight. My hands gripped the vine and I swung myself out onto the water, and as I hit my apex, I let go and for that moment weightlessness overcame my body, and water soon greeted my back as I became submerged. As I resurfaced I was greeted with a warm body up against mine. I blinked through water clouding my sight to find Marilyn's face, smiling in front of mine. I felt a rush all throughout my body from the jump, but that quickly was trumped by the feeling of Marilyn's lips pressed up against mine.

As our kiss ended, we heard a long whistle coming from the branch, as Heath was watching on. My eyes were transfixed on Marilyn's, as the moment held my breath in suspension until the rush of water roared again from Heath landing right next to us. Marilyn proceeded to splash me in the face, and make her way to the branch yet again. We must have jumped five or six more times, and when we became tired we all exited the water onto the slim stretch of sand that ran along the edge.

"You are more than welcome to have one of the hammocks. There are a ton of them on the other side of the pond," Brittany pointed over and I could barely make out the trees connected by them in the distance. Marilyn and I made our way back over and found our clothes, and we put them back on with a slower pace than we removed them, and took each other in. I put my pants back on, and I found a slight discomfort coming from my pocket. Marilyn's eyes widened as I raised a small vial out of my pocket.

As we made our way to the other side of the pond, I held the vial tight in my right hand. *No better time than now.* We struggled to get into the hammock, but eventually rocked back and forth enjoying the nice cool marine air. I held the vial up, and took out the small cork enclosure.

"Let me go with you!" Marilyn grabbed my hand, and gave me a concerned look. I nodded back at her and handed her the vial. She proceeded to drink about half, and I finished the rest. The red liquid had no taste, but I could feel it making its way down my throat, with no recoil. I sat for a minute, staring directly up in front of me. All of a sudden, Marilyn threw her arms up in front of her, and gasped. As I looked over at her, her eyes were rolling into the back of her head, and she became motionless.

"Marilyn!" my yelling echoed into the now empty forest, and my heart raced with panic yet again. I put my ear towards her mouth, and then to her chest. *She's not breathing, she has no heartbeat.* I adjusted myself to try to perform CPR, but as I raised myself up my eyesight became blurry, my senses became muted, and my world became black.

21

As I came to, I was in front a very familiar set of white, marble stairs. With a rush of air and a sudden weight, I felt Marilyn jump on my back with her arms around me.

"What happened?" I shook my head in disbelief, and simply hugged her back. "You became lifeless, your eyes rolled into the back of your head and you were gone, and as I got up to see if I could help you the same thing happened to me," recalling the situation out loud frightened me a bit, and I had to sit down on the stairs and regain my senses. I looked behind me at the large set of stairs in front of me, and I knew where I was, and where I needed to go. "Come on Marilyn," I grabbed her hand and made the trek up yet again. When we surfaced, we heard voices coming from the right side of the hallway, and we quickly made it to a room with the almighty simply sitting at a desk, staring out at us.

"Hello!" I ran over to him, but as I went to embrace him my hand went through his shoulder with no physical contact being registered. Marilyn had her hand at her mouth, and motioned for me to come back over to her.

"Look Ted," she pointed on the desk with two files, and as I slowly made my way behind him once again, I could barely make out what the files said. *Ted Wall. Mary Ann Wall.* My heart raced, and I didn't even get words out to Marilyn before a familiar face joined the room.

"You called sir," Chad saluted him as he walked in.

"Yes, Chad, I need to get word out to both these people as soon as I can; take these please." He handed Chad two gold sealed envelopes, and my mind remembered the look the second Chad received them.

Marilyn and I exchanged no words, but as Chad left, the room went white and there was a rush of air around both of us. The next place we were manifested into was one of the first I could remember, and I saw myself standing in line as Chad got coffee and cookies, and I filled out a piece of paper. *There she is.* Mary Ann was entering the room as Chad walked back over to me, and I raced over to her. Again, my embrace was met with no physical contact, and I was left to be a spectator of our narrow miss. Just as Chad was leading me out of the room after I had submitted my paperwork, a door opened behind the counter. *No, not him.* I watched as Ted walked over and ushered Mary Ann through the door, and again the air rushed around us, and the piercing white light came again.

When we came to, my mind panicked at the location where we had arrived. My first reaction was to embrace Marilyn and offer protection, as the fire lit torches and dark walls surrounded us. Behind us we saw a light, and The Almighty himself once again emerged from the darkness, and was walking briskly to a familiar fire lit room I was not yet two days removed from. We briskly followed behind as the doors swung open, and Ted was sitting, glass in hand at the other side of the room.

"How dare you, I was granted supreme access," he got right in Ted's face, and Ted didn't budge at all.

"Oh, old friend, you know how this all works, and it's been working this way for a long, long time," he threw back a drink in his face, and smiled as he swallowed.

"Supreme access lets me grant words to them first, and you did not allow that, and I am here to make sure words are shared." Ted threw his hands up in protest, but pointed to the other side of the room.

"If it really means that much to you, she's around the corner to the right." Another rush of air passed us as he worked out of the room with haste, and a soft déjà vu came over me as I raced behind him.

What I witnessed both warmed my soul but left me breathless, as I stood at the edge of the same cell I had been to not long ago, watching the embrace of the man who had shown me so much love, and the woman who had as well. Mary Ann spoke furiously, but Marilyn and I couldn't make out any of the words. He put his hands on both sides oh her head, and kissed her forehead. He then went on to bless her, as her head hung down; he was forming the cross over her. I felt a chill go down my spine as Ted was standing right behind me, and as he walked toward them his body went right through mine.

"Enough! Come along now." When Ted spoke Mary Ann looked up at him with a mix of anger and sadness in her eyes, and once again the white light and air rushed alongside us, and we were transported yet again.

As we came to once again, we were in the exact location we stood just a couple of moments ago, with The Almighty sitting with a concerned look on his face. The files remained on his desk, and no words were spoken as the tension gripped the air. His eyes widened and a small smile hit his lips as a woman entered the room, and they shared an embrace. *Mom.* My mother's soft features looked tired and weathered as she sat across from him, and he wasted no time discussing the situation at hand.

"He is going to need help. The amount of discomfort and stress coming is a lot for someone to handle alone." My mother nodded as he continued. "I am going to have you sit as part of The Hope, it will be nice to have familiar faces for him as the trial begins." She once again nodded, but a tear came down her right cheek, and she quickly wiped it away.

"Were you able to talk to Mary Ann?" My mother raised the same concern I felt inside, and a response was needed to ease the worry.

"I was able to speak with her, and she understands the situation, I told her to stay strong and to hang in there, and before he ushered me away I was able to give her my blessing," his words hung in the air as he described his interaction, and as I looked at Marilyn her eyes were fixated on the conversation. My mother stood up, and embraced him once again. He put both hands on the sides of her head, and seemed to speak the same words as he had blessed Mary Ann with, and as my mother left the room, the air rushed and the white light took us with it.

22

The hammock was still as my eyes opened, and I looked over at Marilyn and her eyes were staring straight into mine. She rested her head on my chest, and it slowly ascended and descended with every breath I took. The amount of thoughts racing through my mind all at once muted my ability to speak, so I was left suspended in a fabric swing. After what seemed like hours, Marilyn lifted her head up and sat up in the hammock, and stretched her arms out. She turned to look back at me, and when her eyes met mine she smiled, as she knew in that moment what my look meant. I had to go back.

The darkness never subsided during the whole time we were deep in this forest, but as our trek back drew nearer to the tracks light started to filter through. I kept my head down, my legs moving forward, determined to fully understand the depth of my situation, and as I looked behind me, Marilyn was keeping pace step by step. When we reached the tracks, there was no train to be seen and I jumped down in one swift motion as Marilyn made her way down after. Marilyn and I resurfaced on the other side and as I went to go back to my room her hand met my shoulder.

"Ted, I'll go back now, tell them we are going forward with the trial, why don't you go get cleaned up and I will meet you back here." As she finished speaking I leaned in only to be met with her index finger on my lips. She smiled, and casually made her way back to the loading station and was on her way.

I re-entered the building and darted over towards a hallway I hadn't been in a long time, and made my way into a bar that had beckoned me when I first arrived here. I scanned the room and finally met eyes with the wise, skittish man I had met a few days ago. I made my way over, and was greeted with a hug from him.

"Hello old friend, come sit, I'll roll another." Despite his invitation, I knew time was of the essence, so I politely declined.

"Hunter, I have come to say hello and goodbye, and I would like you to know something…" as I rambled on about the village in the woods he scribbled notes on the bar napkin sitting by his side. He saluted me, gave me a hug, and I made my way back to my room.

I found myself pacing back and forth in my room, trying to dissect and organize all the thoughts in my head. As I prepared myself physically for the trial with the appropriate clothing and outer look, the mental side of me was completely panicked and in shock. *My calculations put this trial with hell leading three to two.*

The idea of being in the dark abyss forever never fully left my mind, even though I had been born and raised optimistic by my mother and the people I had always surrounded myself with. I continued to pace as the same strip of carpet got the brunt of my attention, until I heard a knock on the door. Marilyn made her way in.

"Ted, they are ready for you," her demeanor was very calm yet concerning, as my gut feelings radiated out of her as well. We made the walk outside slow and meticulous, and when we made our way to the station I couldn't help but take in all the shades of blue in the sky around me. After what seemed like days in darkness my eyes welcomed the sight of light and color. As I took in the beauty of the canvas in front of me, my eyes met the beautiful hue that was Marilyn's eyes, and even in a time of complete chaos, the simplest things calmed my nerves.

When we boarded the train, an attendant walked over to me. He simply reached out his hand and dropped two gold coins in mine, and walked away.

"Sir, what are these for?" He smirked and looked back at me.

"After today, you may need them if you would like to board this train again." His voice hung in the car as I processed the information, and once again my heart raced at the thought of what was to come.

Marilyn and I did not exchange any words on the ride over, but I was greeted with a warm reception when I returned to the entrance of the theater. My mind shot back memories of Ted swallowing me in fire and his red eyes levitating towards me, and I had to steady my breathing before sitting down. I sat in angst as I waited for both parties to arrive on stage, and I must have looked back at Marilyn twenty times waiting for what was next. The doors on both sides swung open, and seven familiar faces walked out. *Where is my mother?*

My nerves struck up again as a silence fell over the room, and the absence of my mother was brief as she made her way in from the middle of stage, and stood in the middle facing us.

"Hello, and welcome back to the trial of Ted Wall, my son." Instantly tears filled my eyes as I took in her love through her eyes. "Today, the topic of discussion is Sloth. Sloth is a sin of all states; mental, spiritual, emotional and physical. When one is does not value time, it becomes wasted. The Hope you may begin," her soft voice carried so well as the rest of the theater was completely silent. She sat down, took a deep breath, and a screen dropped in the theater once again.

23

"I don't think I have ever taken a vacation this long before! You are going to have to coach me through it." Mary Ann gripped my hand as the landing gear of the plane rumbled beneath us.

"I am just glad we did an all-inclusive. It makes it so much easier to just be able to eat and drink at the same location all week." My words were slightly slurred due to the liquid meal I had on the plane, but Mary Ann understood what my point was.

"We owe my parents for the rest of our lives after this surprise, I honestly didn't even plan a honeymoon, I kind of thought buying a house would suffice as a good enough life moment after marriage." She smiled as the thought of our home we were going to return to, as a newly married couple.

We were greeted with a string of flowers around our necks as we deplaned, and we were quickly ushered to a compound straight out of the advertisements you see on television. The water was transparent and the most beautiful shade of blue, and the palm trees speckled the landscape all around us, I was in heaven.

Mary Ann and I made our way to the bar, and our feet couldn't decide where the bar floor began and where the beach ended. When we looked at the board behind the bar, there were a total of one hundred different themed cocktails.

As we scanned the board the bartender yelled out at us, "How long are you here for?" In my sober state of mind I simply stated that I was never leaving. He had a good laugh and said the most beautiful seven words I had ever heard. "Why don't you try all of them?" Mary Ann looked over at me with a determination in her eyes, and slammed her fist down on the bar in compliance. The bar let out a holler, and the bartender began making us the first and second cocktail on the menu. "One bay breeze for you, and one island sunset for you!" The drinks were pieces of art, and despite my wanting to keep the beauty intact, the drinks were drained quickly. When the bartender told me 'deep blue sea' was drink number eleven, the night started to slowly fall out of memory.

A warm breeze blanketed my body as my eyes opened slowly one at a time, and despite a physical protest I raised my head to assess my surroundings. The sun was peeking up on the horizon as I caught a glimpse of an angel walking through the dim light. Mary Ann's slender figure didn't even seem to touch the ground as she passed through my line of sight, and I was soon joined by a warm body void of clothing next to me, and as Mary Ann's head rested on my chest my eyes closed I was once again at peace. The next time my eyes opened the sun was fully ablaze, and I was ready to get the day started.

Mary Ann sat in an oversized chair on the deck facing the ocean, and our conversation about the day was short and sweet. "I have nothing planned Ted, maybe some food, a massage followed by a nap, and back to the bar to continue our one hundred step program." I had no problem agreeing to her set of plans, and simply shook my head and greeted her with a kiss.

The next several days seemed to blend together as we stocked up on mixed drinks and an overabundance of sleep. Other than the occasional videoconference with her parents and a couple of jealous friends, the time spent was as peaceful and serene as we could spend it. I overheard a long haired gentleman at the bar proclaim, "Nothing is something worth doing!" which made me laugh out loud, as that was sworn in as the motto for this whole trip. The bartender not only knew us by name when our last night arrived, he had nicknames for us.

"Well, looks like number fifty is going to be the last drink. Although you only made it half way, I must say I am impressed, especially regrouping after the first night put you down for the count." He handed us our drinks and we laughed with him as the memories of the week poured into recent memory. I didn't have words for Mary Ann in that moment; I just sat and looked at her. She was perfect, and it was effortless. In a way, it frustrated me how much one person could care and not care so seamlessly, and still have a ton of love in her heart. I had been with her for four years to this day, and married for seven days, but in that moment, I fell in love for the first time all over again.

The theater illuminated all around me and I could hear the soft sounds of sobs surrounding me. The image of her on that trip and her locked in the cell vied for attention at the forefront of my mind. My mother looked back at me with a smile on her face, as she stood up and made herself present in front of us all again. As the room got quiet and became still again, I saw her walk over to Ted. Although the exchange they shared was brief, I could tell the words exchanged were heated, as the body language became primal with Ted rising to his feet at the end. I found myself standing and wanting to make my way to the stage, but my mother put her hand out and signaled for me to remain, and she cued the lights and the screen once again. As the Circle's rebuttal drew near, the adrenaline pumping through me made my vision narrow, but the calm smile radiated in front of me and the pair of hands consoling me on my shoulders brought me back down, and I settled in again.

"Come in please Ted." I could never decipher what my boss needed or wanted by the tone of his voice, as his sarcasm in the office was thrown around ad nauseam. I sat down without saying a word, trying to judge whether his tone was serious or not, as his facial expression remained still.

"Thank you for coming Ted," he opened a folder as he addressed me, and feeling of concern consumed me. "Our company on a corporate level has decided to merge with another company, Ohio Telecom. After a brief consulting by our new partners, they have decided that slimming down the workforce would be the best way to spare costs in the immediate future, and..." as he continued I found myself standing up and making my way over to the window as the snow came down. "Ted." I put my hand out to silence him. Self-doubt and anger filled me.

"Making a company better by removing the workforce to save money," I shook my head as I paced back and forth in my boss's oversized office.

"In due time, when positions become available," he stuttered and got choked up as he continued, and I flung my chair across the room with one swift motion.

"Kiss my ass!" I still couldn't tell on my way out what the true emotion in my boss was, but the drive to the bar was one of the quickest on record.

"Hello Ted, seems a bit early to be seeing you here," I raised two fingers at Paul and he quickly retrieved a glass and filled it. My adrenaline soothed the burn as it went down, and every cell in my body instantly eased and I sank into the stool.

"Just do me a favor Paul, just don't let me see through the bottom of this glass." He nodded and went on to fill my glass again, as each drink had me remembering followed by a quick forget. My eyes became fixated on the football game on the television as the snow made it hard for the players to even keep their footing on the field. Fans near me hoot and hollered as the teams traded scoring possessions. My phone vibrated in my pocket as the backlit screen informed me my wife was trying to reach me.

"Hey honey what's up?" I articulated every word the best I could poorly hiding my whereabouts.

"Ted, it is nine thirty, I have been trying to reach you since six, where have you been?" The realization of time sobered me up instantly as five hours had passed me by so quickly.

"I am down the street, just had a couple of drinks, want to join me?" I felt like that transition was as smooth as it could have been.

"I have to be back at the hospital by six, I am going to bed," the phone clicked off, and I became frustrated at the idea of my wife being mad at me the day I was let go to save costs, I motioned to Paul once again.

"Ted, it has been months since you lost your job, you have to start making progress and you have to find a job, I can only support the both of us for so much time," her words were muted to my ears as I moved the food around on my plate.

"I have calls out, and this whole entire city has my resume Mary Ann. As I have said before, my line of work no longer exists in this city," my words thrashed out, and they became instantly aggressive.

"The hospital is preparing to promote me to head nurse, and here I am dealing with my unemployed husband," her words whipped at my back, and the sting burned to the bone.

"Mary Ann, I changed jobs for you. I changed the city I lived in for you, and I changed my whole entire life for you, I just need more time to assess." She gave me a brief look of sympathy but quickly rolled her eyes, and grabbed the bottle of wine and her glass.

"My award dinner is set for six tomorrow, and they are announcing my promotion at seven, please don't be late," her footsteps rang down the hall, and the door to the bedroom slammed shut.

"I just don't understand Paul, how quickly things can change, one moment I am working full time celebrating my third Christmas as a married couple in my home with my white picket fence, and now I am jobless and struggling to hang onto the coattails of my wife." Paul shook his head as he buffed glasses behind the bar.

"There are only nine thousand people in this town Ted, and everyone knows you. If there was a job I am sure you would be the first person that would get a call, but the opportunity just doesn't present itself that often." His words made so much sense I felt sick, but continued to cloud my reason with thoughts of the past. "There has to be a way, something else I can do, I am sure I will be able to find it." The whiskey went from cold to hot as it entered my mouth and made its way down my throat.

"Can't believe Cleveland lost again, I swear we are cursed!" Paul's proclamation shot a bolt of terror through my body.

"Paul, what time is it?" I shuffled on the stool to find the answer, but Paul quickly gave me the bad news I wasn't hoping for.

"Ted, it's eight thirty."

I didn't even bother driving to the hospital due to the time, but as I approached the house I found myself driving by but not pulling in. After slowly passing four or five times, I pulled into the driveway and quickly turned my lights off. I sat in the car taking in all the warmth that I could that was pumping out of the vents before I entered the cold winter air. Every step I took, snow crunched underneath my feet and I had to struggle to remain stable due to the hidden ice and liquid digesting in my body. An eerie silence hung in the air as I opened the front door and couldn't sense the whereabouts of anyone in the house. I peeked around the kitchen and saw nothing out in the open, as if no one had been home the whole day. As I took a couple steps up the stairs I heard a mumbled expletive coming from the living room.

"Mary Ann?" I walked over and saw her sitting on the couch, in the darkness.

"Deep down I knew you would forget, but I wanted to see if I could be proved wrong," I had never heard this tone out of her, and a mixture of anger and sadness boiled within. "My whole life I have been working for this night, and during the most hard earned thirty minutes of my professional career my husband was not there. He was continuing his sulking and lost track of time." Her statements lashed out at me, and I couldn't muster any words.

"Columbus is full of sales positions Ted, I am sure you will find one there," I walked over and sat next to her, but she didn't look towards me. "Mary Ann, you just got promoted, you can't move to Columbus," my realization crept from within, and somehow I knew it had been lying dormant for months. "Ted, I am talking about you going alone."

As the lights slowly came back on my body filled with frustration, as the personal level of the trial was truly starting to get to me. *I don't think I am a bad person, what if some of these were just misunderstandings.* I rubbed my face with both hands over and over until my skin became mildly numb. I turned around to see a concerned Marilyn staring back, as in a few moments I could face my eternal fate, and here I was sitting with a frustrated mindset created because of a conversation between Mary Ann and me. I had trouble forming anything worthy of conversation for Marilyn, and she just took my head in her arms and ran her fingers through my hair.

"It'll be okay, I'm sure of it," she rocked back and forth and exuded a quiet confidence that soothed the moment. I heard a soft hum coming from her, and I was barely able to recognize it. *Twenty-One Pilots?* I lifted my head and smiled at her, acknowledging her choice. "Love that song Ted, but way too overplayed," I laughed out loud at the brutal honesty, and shifted my focus to the stage as everyone was making their way back out. My mother made her way to the middle of the stage, and Ted remained leaning up against the wall by the door.

"The decision has been made…" as my mother spoke the door slammed and Ted was nowhere to be seen, and as she continued The Circle got up and quickly followed behind. "Ted honey, you are coming with me tonight." Mother smiled and motioned for me to come up on the stage, and as my hand met hers the room faded away.

24

When I could register where I was, I could smell fresh marine air and every breath I took seemed to revitalize me. My mother was beside me smiling, and her skin glowed with the same energy I remember from when I was young. She took my hand and we started walking down a winding street filled with thick pine trees and the sound of water right behind. I tried to muster up questions to ask but every time I muttered a sound my mother gave me a look that told me to stay quiet, and that is what I did. The houses on each side of the road were very ornate, with architecture resembling nothing that I had ever seen. From the outside I was estimating there must be an average of six or seven bedrooms in these houses, with large outside areas littered with trees and beautiful green grass to contrast. My mother walked us down past about ten or so houses, and took a slight right into a long driveway, with a large house approaching in the distance. When the porch in the front of house came into view, my heart began to race and I felt a tingle of sweet recognition from my fingers to my toes. *I know all these people.*

My cousin Esther came racing off the porch and jumped into my arms, and I squeezed her with all my might, involuntary tears streaming out of my eyes. As our embrace ended, I started to recognize all the faces sitting in front of me, and I didn't know where to start.

"Hello Grandma." I was having trouble forming complete sentences as I embraced her, and her grip was so strong on my back. I kissed her and looked at the full gallery, and simply bowed and saluted, and everyone clapped and began to embrace me one by one. My uncle Larry, my grandfather Frank, my cousins Erin and Denise. My soul was overflowing with every exchange of hellos years in the making, and my mind had trouble taking in the full situation I was in.

"Come on, let's go inside," my mother said as she grabbed my arm, and I followed her into the kitchen. As we walked in the house it struck a chord of similarity in the way the interior was laid out, with the large set of stairs in the front, and the open concept on the main level that gave sight access to the front and back of the house. My mother walked up the stairs, and I didn't hesitate to follow as the hallway extended on both sides, and rooms were laid out one after another.

"Grandma and Grandpa, cousin Esther, cousin Erin, Uncle Larry..." one after another she showed me each room, and the realization of where I was started to dawn on me.

"Mom, you are all here together," my words were simplistic, but she smiled back at me with a glow in her eyes.

"As we should be Ted, I requested it to be this way," she continued as it dawned on me that she was the first to pass away at such a young age, and everyone I met passed away after her. She got to the end of the hallway and opened a door, and motioned for me to enter. The room was large, with deep brown wood walls, a rug to soften the blow of hard wood steps underfoot, and a bed large enough for five. "Whose room is this?" I looked back at her and was simply greeted with a smile from her as she leaned up against the doorway.

"Ted, honey this is your room, if you would like to make it yours." I ran my hand along the bed frame, and made my way over to the window on the far side of the room. The window exited out onto an overhang that hung over the porch in the front, and I took a deep breath. My mother's hand greeted my back, and I met her teary eyes.

"But Ted honey, it will be waiting for you, whenever that time may come," she walked out of the room and back down the hall, and I followed her after slowly closing the door behind me, barely making a sound.

The commotion in the kitchen came to a standstill as my mother and I entered, and she motioned her hand for everyone to carry on. She weaved through the people and was making her way to the back deck, and after multiple more hugs and kisses, I could be at her side once again. I looked out into the back, and saw a still formation of water present, and felt a tinge of remembrance as she began to speak again.

"Ted, I have to tell you a couple of things, I would have earlier if I had the opportunity," her stern face stilled me, and my focus was completely with her. "Do you remember the night the accident happened?" the way she asked the question seized me, and it took me a second to rebalance my memories.

"I...don't," despite all the deepest thinking I could muster, nothing came to me.

"Honey, you will learn of your fate tomorrow night, and you must know the situation you are in," she looked away from me, tears coming down from her eyes.

"I am ready, please mom," I put my arm around her, and after a few quick sobs, she relaxed herself and spoke softly.

"You were with Mary Ann, and you got into a car accident. Due to the circumstances that preceded, Mary Ann would not have been granted a trial, but an exception was made. Ted took Mary Ann before details were shared with her, and she has been trapped since." Her words stuck to my heart, and a mixture of anger and confusion settled in.

"Mom, what will happen to her?" Her eyes radiated through the tears, and she took a deep breath. "This whole trial was to decide the fate of both of you, not just you Ted."

My mind went blank, and I gripped the wooden rail of the deck with both hands. Every single memory I could muster of the recent interactions raced through my mind, and words were hard to form.

"The Almighty came to me, and asked me to be part of The Hope and to assist in picking the memories of your defense," I stared at her, with love filling my heart. "He also asked me to find someone to help you through it, and I knew Marilyn would be the right one. It took me a while to locate her, but after a bit of convincing she agreed to it, and I would say it has worked out so far." She smiled while my memory of our physical connection ignited my body, and I mustered a soft chuckle at my recollections.

"Why Marilyn?" My question sat in the air for a couple of minutes before she answered my question.

"I needed someone that would match the amount of love you give and shares the intense amount of optimism you have always had, and she fit the bill. All I have ever wanted for you was love and happiness Ted. Marilyn demonstrated both of those qualities so effortlessly, and she stood to gain from this assistance as well."

I pondered that thought, and had to prod back.

"What exactly did she stand to gain?" My mother knew the question was coming, and answered back quickly. "Well, a couple of things Ted. First, she gets a good-looking man to hang out with and share time with. Second, she mustered up the courage to exit that village she was living in the forest, and be able to bring the amazing energy back for others to bask in and to find life in," she stalled, and ran her fingers through her hair. My sole focus was on my mother, and every word made me feel more alive. "Finally, I told her I would sit as part The Hope for her, if she reconvened with her personal trial."

I hugged my mom with as much energy as I could muster and as I looked back towards the house every family member watched on as tears came down their faces in unison.

"It took a lot of convincing Ted, she was reluctant to go back, she was afraid. Deep down I think you have helped her as much as she has helped you, you two make quite the pair," she laughed out loud a little and again my memories of our pond interactions filled my mind, and I couldn't help but blush. "Ted, you deserved so much more, the amount of energy you gave in your life was unmatched by anyone you came in contact with." A slight hint of frustration in her voice became noticeable, and she quickly silenced her thoughts from rambling on. We stood there for a moment, and basked in the twilight in the distance. She guided me back inside and let everyone swarm me yet again. After filling my soul with all the long lost unconditional love that the house brought, she guided me back to the front porch and down onto the long driveway.

As we approached the end of the driveway, light started to filter through the trees, and our shadows lengthened in front of us. We slowly came to a stop, and stared into each other's eyes.

"Do me a favor Ted, tell Marilyn good luck for me, big day for her tomorrow," I tilted my head sideways as this new information registered, and nodded to accept the favor. "Stay strong honey, you have done so well so far, and I have no doubt you will continue to show resilience. Tomorrow is a big day, take it in stride, and stay optimistic like you have always been." I hugged her again, and stood still for a good two minutes.

"I missed you so much mom, I miss you every day." I put my hand on her cheek as she mustered a smile.

"I never wanted to leave you Ted, but everyone has his or her time, and there is no perfect way to go," she grabbed my hand in hers. "I love you son," my hand heated, as we remained connected.

"I love you too mom." I turned and walked back towards where this night had started, and as the light began to flood the sky my world melted, and the eve of my verdict faded away.

25

My eyes opened to a familiar sight, and once again I lay in the same bed where I awoke from the last six verdicts, and as I got up and made the bed, I realized in that moment I would not be returning. When my feet started to direct me around my room, I noticed a small white sliver peeking out from the bottom of the door. I picked up the two pieces of paper and began to examine them.

> *Congratulations for making it this far, and best wishes for the future. Hopefully your final verdict graces you with eternal happiness and pleasure. As you depart we please ask you to fill out this brief survey so we can better serve those who will soon learn their fate after you. Best wishes, Chad.*

I couldn't help but laugh out loud, and soon wonder where the chocolates on the pillows and the complimentary massages have been this whole time. I shuffled the paper underneath the other, and found a more simple and concise message.

> *Down the hall, take a left. Room eleven. Marilyn.*

I took a deep breath and tried to control the anxiety gripping me, as three fates would be resolved today. When the shower water hit my skin, I couldn't help but rub my muscles to try to alleviate the stress I had been holding the whole time I had been here. When the mirror granted me my reflection through the condensation that had covered it, I stared at myself. *Car accident. Mary Ann. Room with my mom. Marilyn's trial.*

My mind was moving a mile a minute, and all I could do was continue to groom myself to keep my physical being well distracted.

I grabbed a black suit from the closet, and scanned through the ties. *My mom said orange always calmed me as a child.* The orange stood brilliant up against the black shirt and black coat I had put on. I walked around the room, ran my hand along the bed, and made my way to the door. As I opened the door I looked back, turned out the light, and made my way.

Room eleven was only a little way down, and when I went to knock on it the door stood ajar, and I eased the door backward. Although I did not see anyone at first, only the soft melody of Paul Simon and Art Garfunkel cascaded through the room. I scanned the room and coming up empty I made my way to the bathroom.

"Marilyn!" I ran over and sat down next to her, as she had her knees pressed to her chest and tears streamed down her eyes.

"I don't think I can do it," her words limped out of her mouth, and though my fear was on the forefront of my mind, I stayed calm.

"Marilyn, I have no doubt in my mind you will be okay today," my optimism was my strongest attribute, and I always wondered why other people had such a hard time exuding it.

"Will you do me a favor Ted," her eyes pierced me, I nodded. "Will you go first today?" the question caused the hair on the back of my neck stand up, and I nodded reluctantly after a quick contemplation. I helped her to her feet, and as she got ready no more words were exchanged.

She came out of the bathroom donning white dress, white pearls around her neck and red lipstick that could melt the room. I smiled and extended my arm out and hooked her elbow, and without much hesitation she turned the lights off and we were again on our way. With each step we took I took careful notice of the breaths I was taking, urging on a calm demeanor that was masking complete chaos deep down. We stood for a second in the lobby and took in the surroundings, and as people walked past us it was like no one even knew, and everyone just carried on their business as usual. *Just another day.* I saluted back towards the main area, turned and made my way out the door. A soft glow filled the space around us with the smell of smoke and fallen leaves filled the air. When we approached the train station it stood idle, and the conductor was standing at our entrance.

"Welcome, I wish you both luck and best wishes," he extended his hand out and Marilyn proceeded to fill his hand with two gold coins, and after recognizing the gesture I followed suit.

"What was that all about Marilyn?" I sat with confusion building up.

"The coins allow passage for our soul to travel. I was told about it a long time ago, and have been holding on to the coins since. There is no turning back now." Her words gripped me, and held me firm against my seat. *No turning back.*

As we exited the train, I tried to muster words of encouragement and optimism but I was left dry. My mind had shifted focus towards what was to come, and by process of elimination I knew what was about to manifest before me.

"Marilyn, what sin will ultimately decide your fate?" She peered back at me with contempt, and cleared her throat.

"Lust," she said shaking her head and smiling a bit as she looked down at the ground. "You still think I will be okay?" She stopped and looked at me, and without thinking I responded the best that I could.

"I have no doubt, and hopefully, I will see you again, I can't imagine it any other way." She smiled and hugged me, and with a quick kiss on the check, we entered the location of our final fate. Hanging overhead as we entered was the same familiar marquee, this time two names hung, Ted Wall and Marilyn Monroe.

As the doors to the theater opened, the sound of applause filled the room. Every seat in the whole entire theater was filled, and all of the spectators were on their feet. I looked out towards the stage and saw The Hope, including my mother, all applauding our entrance. All four members of The Circle sat idle, staring forward, and I looked back and motioned Marilyn to look at them.

"They are going to miss out on two souls today," My words seemed to calm her, and her eyes couldn't help but touch every set in the whole entire packed theater. I sat down in the chair, front and center and reminded myself to breathe, as the air seemed to be running thin in the room. There was a long, lingering calm as everyone became still, and a familiar face donned the stage. For the second time in about fifteen minutes, the whole room erupted with applause, and the figure standing in front of us bowed, and motioned for silence. When the room became quiet again, he turned around and motioned at the curtain. Slowly making her way from behind the curtain Mary Ann walked out, eyes fixated on the ground. Ted shuffled in his chair as he watched The Almighty himself embrace her, and display her for all the spectators to see.

The Almighty proceeded. "Welcome back to the trial of Ted Wall, where we will decide two fates today." A collective gasp could be heard around the theater, including a very audible one from Marilyn right behind me. My mother and I connected with our eyes, and she nodded back at me reconfirming the information she shared with me the night before.

"After the sin has been fully examined and displayed, there will be a fifteen-minute deliberation, and we will reconvene for final verdict," you could hear a pin drop as he spoke, and I again reminded myself to breathe, and stay calm. "The topic of discussion today is Wrath, where one spurns love and opts for fury. There should always be a balance between our physical, mental and emotional state, yet when wrath is involved the balance is thrown off entirely. We are going to begin with The Hope." He finished and walked over with Mary Ann towards where my mother was sitting, greeted her, and he and Mary Ann took their seats right next to her. My eyes remained locked on Mary Ann, and as her eyes lifted from the ground, they momentarily met mine before the screen dropped yet again.

26

When I looked down at the speedometer and realized I was going twenty over, I had to force my foot to ease off the pedal. The excitement surging through my body was not subsiding, as I couldn't wait to tell my parents about the engagement that had just occurred just twelve hours ago. I told Mary Ann I was going to take the day off to drive to tell them, and promised not to post on social media until the whole entire family was informed over the phone or in person. When I pulled into the driveway I barely put the car in park before I was hopping out. I leapt up the porch stairs, rang the doorbell and was greeted with a stalemate. The door was locked, and despite my knocking and ringing, no one was coming. My adrenaline pumped furiously through my body, and I found myself calling my parents on the phone from the front porch.

"Open the door!" My adrenaline was giving way to frustration as I left three word voicemails. I heard a faint noise coming from the garage, and as the door lifted my father's car backed up, and despite my waving and yelling, he was gone.

I entered the house through the garage and quickly scanned every room on the main level only to find the house completely empty. I went up the stairs and crept around to my parent's bedroom. Words can't describe the emotion that runs through a body when you see your own mother crying, and as I entered her room I quickly made my way over to her.

"Mom, what's wrong?" I grabbed her as she continued to sob and she couldn't produce words for a couple of minutes. When she settled herself down, her bloodshot eyes met mine.

"Ted honey, what a nice surprise, I didn't expect to see you, what are you doing here?" her calm demeanor threw me off, and I hesitated with my news.

"Mom, why are you so upset? I saw dad leave in a hurry, what's going on?" She began to cry again, and I stood up and paced a bit in the room.

"Come downstairs," she said as she got up and quickly exited the room. I followed with haste. There was an envelope on the table, and its contents were spilled out onto the table. My mother leaned back up against the counter, and motioned for me to pick up the papers. After a brief overview, I was having a hard time understanding the full picture. I dropped the paper on the table and raised my arms towards my mom, who took a deep breath and returned the worst three-word combination in the English language. "I have cancer."

The frustration and adrenaline that had built up inside my body subsided and made way for sadness and confusion. I cried involuntarily, and my mother walked over to console me.

"My consultation with the doctor is tomorrow, if you want to come." I nodded towards her, and embraced her again.

"Mom, where did dad go?" She backed away from me and walked back over to the counter where she was before.

"He didn't take the news very well Ted." She stared at the ground as the information settled in.

"So where did he go?" I felt a bit of anger build up inside of me as the question left my lips.

"I don't know honey, but he'll come back, he always does." Her words carried little life as they left her, and at that moment I had forgotten the reason why I had even made this trip, as Mary Ann's phone call vibrated in my pocket.

"Hey there…" Mom stood still as I spoke.

"Hey Ted! Did you tell your parents yet?" her voice amplified in the room, and my mother perked up.

"No, not yet, I just got here." My lie was met by the glaring eyes of my mother, who had mustered up a smile for the first time since I had gotten there.

"Well, let me know how it goes!" Her excitement radiated through me.

"Will do honey, love you." My mother walked towards me as I hung up the phone.

"Congratulations son!" She hugged me and gave me as much love as she could muster, and I soaked it all in.

The sky was a deep shade of grey as the rain came pouring down, and I assisted my mother over some puddles as we made our way into the clinic. During the mild wait, my mother and I didn't exchange any words about the state of her being or my father's noticeable absence from the doctor visit.

"We are ready for you now," said the nurse as she guided us back, and we sat waiting for the doctor in his office. We greeted the doctor as he arrived and he sat down with my mother's file in front of him.

"I don't like this part of the job, I really don't." I could sense the stress of the conversation was weighing on him, and the mood in the room became quite somber. "The cancer originated in your kidneys, and it has since spread to your liver and your pancreas. After an examination, I believe with chemotherapy treatment you can expect to live about a year. If you forego treatment we are looking at around three months." His hesitation sucked the air and life out of the room, and all three of us remained silent.

"Thank you doctor." My mother and I got up and quickly walked out of the room. Our drive home was quick due to the lack of cars driving through the storm, and the car idled in the driveway as I put it in park.

"I'll be back mom, go inside." She glanced at me and tried to protest, but she knew it wouldn't make a difference. She kissed me on the cheek, and as she got into the house, I put the car in reverse.

I sat outside of the local bar for a good thirty minutes conjuring up the courage to walk in, as every negative emotion flooded my body. The smoky interior of the bar hit me like a wall as I made my way inside. I scanned the length of the bar, and despite having no windows offering any natural light; I spotted a lone man sitting at the end of the bar.

"What in the hell do you think you are doing here?" I raised my voice a bit as I made my way towards him, and he just threw up a hand in protest. I grabbed his shoulder, and turned him around so he could face me. "I asked you a question." I couldn't register the emotion behind his eyes as he stared at me.

"Your mother has cancer son," his words enraging me even more.

"I was there, I was trying to get your attention, I took her to the hospital!" I slammed my fist on the bar as he cowered away. "What is your problem? She just sat there and cried and had to muster up the courage to go to the doctor without your support, and here you are drinking your sorrows away." My anger was building, and his calm demeanor was not helping.

"Ted, you wouldn't understand. There is more to the situation that you don't know," he sipped his drink as his smug comment left his lips.

"I just sat with her as a doctor told her she had a year left if she was lucky, so tell me dad, what don't I understand?" My eyes never left him, and the lone patrons in the bar remained quiet and still.

"She doesn't have life insurance Ted, and there is no way we can get it now."

I grabbed his shoulder and threw him to the floor. As he hit his glass broke behind him, and glass poured out onto the ground. I reared back and laid my right fist so hard across his jaw I felt teeth crack underneath my knuckles. As I cocked back with my left fist I put my body into it and again felt his jaw and teeth receive my blow. After another strike with both fists the bartender and another patron at the bar restrained me, and I quickly shrugged them off. I put my hands around my father's throat and stared at him.

"You stay away from her, and you stay away from us. Your negativity makes this whole process worse, and there is no need for it. If I see you again, I won't stop!" Again the bartender pulled me back, and I got to my feet. I leaned over him, and stared into his eyes for the final time. I couldn't gauge the look he gave or emotion he exuded in that moment, but as I walked out of that bar one of the most caustic aspects in my life ceased to be.

"Is there anything I can get for you?" the nurse re-entered the room, and walked over towards me. Fighting through my exhaustion I shook my head, and she smiled and gave me a blanket. I rubbed my eyes and looked at my mother, and the sight of tubes coming from her skin and machines detecting vitals released my anxiety again. I began to stare blankly at the door of the hospital room, and was jostled from my daze as my phone vibrated in my pocket.

"Hey honey," I whispered as quietly as I could.

"Hey Ted, how is she?" Mary Ann spoke so affirmatively, being in the medical industry created that vibe.

"She is okay, hanging in there," I lied, but it helped. "I am on my way, I just got out of work, I will stop by the house and I'll be there by the morning. I love you!"

I whispered my love back and hung up the phone. The nurse once again passed, and I quickly got to my feet to meet her.

"Excuse me, is there any way I can get some water?" she nodded, and within a couple of minutes she had returned with some water. "Thank you, what is your name?" She smiled back at me, welcoming the conversation.

"My name is Melanie, nice to meet you." She stuck out her hand and I met it with a formal handshake. "Thank you for everything you have done for my mother." She nodded at my admiration, to show her reception of my sentiment. We stood there together looking on, and the silence weighed heavy in the room. Suddenly, the heart monitor flat lined. Panic and chaos ensued, as Melanie rushed out looking for a doctor and I was left alone. I ran over to Mom, and grabbed her shoulders. I began to shake her, and then wrap my arms around her and I held her as tight as I could. The doctor pried me away and checked her vitals, and without trying to bring her back, she was gone.

As the lights came up, the whole theater was still with the sound of a collective sob coming forth. I kept moving my glance from Mary Ann, to my mother, then to Marilyn behind me looking for consolation and comfort. *This is it.* I raised my head and leaned back a bit, taking a deep breath. *Calm yourself Ted.* The screen remained lowered, the lights again dimmed, and everyone remained completely still in their seats. Ted was shuffling a bit on stage in front of me, releasing some nervous tension I suppose. *Not today, not any day.* My gaze found the screen once again in the middle of the stage, and a countdown began. With each tick that passed, I found a set of eyes to peer into. *Ted. Mom. Marilyn. Mary Ann. Deep breath, here we go.*

"Hey there, it's me, just checking in with you, to see how everything is going. I miss you. I love you. Call me back." I threw the phone onto the bed after leaving the third consecutive voicemail of the day. *Something is up.* Ever since I started the new job in Columbus the amount I was talking to Mary Ann had waned, and the amount I saw Mary Ann had diminished. Our marriage was on life support, and I needed to do something. I cracked a beer and walked down the edge of the parking lot where our community mailbox was. I retrieved a mound of mail, and as I sifted through it most of it founds it way to the trash until I found an envelope with my name handwritten on it, without a return address on the back. It had started to rain and as I made my way over to the closest source of light large drops of water were hitting the paper as I held it up to view what it said. *Mary Ann Wall. August nineteenth. Ted Wall summoned to appear Monday, August twenty-ninth. Irreconcilable differences.* Before I could take in the full information printed before me, I found the rain coming down harder, and ran for cover.

"*You have reached Mary Ann; please leave a message after the tone and I will return your call; thank you.* I held the silent phone to my ear and just found myself breathing into the phone. *If you are satisfied with this message, press five, to re-record, press seven.* I ended the call and threw the phone onto the dining room table and sat down to examine the sheet of paper again. *This is real.* I picked up the phone again and dialed Mary Ann.

"*You have reached Mary Ann, please leave a…*" I slammed the phone on the table, and the screen shattered on impact. I slid it to the other side of the table with the back of my hand, and crossed my arms and sat silently. *No, this can't be how it ends.* I went into my bedroom and changed into a new set of clothes, grabbed my umbrella and stood at my door. I put my forehead against the door, listening to rain on the outside pour down. I opened one eye and spotted my shattered phone, grabbed it and was out the door. The walk from my apartment to my car soaked the front half of my clothes even with the desperate help of my umbrella in the air. I picked up the phone yet again, and heard a familiar four soft rings. *You have reached Mary Ann...* "I am coming to see you Mary Ann, right now. We have to talk." I put the phone in the cup holder between my seats, and put the car in drive.

The highway was empty, and my car was silent. The repetition of my windshield wipers hypnotized me, and as the minutes became hours, I was approaching my destination. Suddenly I heard a ring, and my phone was lighting up with a set of beautiful green eyes looking back at me through the shattered glass. I glided my thumb to the right on the screen to accept the call and the glass slid effortlessly right through my skin, leaving the screen crimson red.

"Hello?" The phone was silent. "Hello?" My body filled with a toxic combination of sadness, anger and frustration.

"Ted," her voice was strained. "ou av urn ond," I couldn't make out what she was saying, and squinted to find my phone held little service on the back roads I was taking.

"Mary Ann, I am on my way to you. We have to talk, tonight," I gingerly pressed the button to end the call, and found my foot pressing harder on the pedal as my car raced around the back-country roads. As I re-entered the main highway, my phone lit up signaling I had received two voicemails. *I am close enough already.* I bypassed them and took the exit; I was only five minutes away.

When I reached the driveway, I was unable to park next to her car because an orange Mustang was parked there, so I parallel parked on the road and ran across the front yard. My haste bypassed a doorbell ring or a knock and I shook myself a little when I got inside to relieve a little bit of the rain I had accumulated.

"Mary Ann!" I peered up the stairs and into the living room only to find them vacant. When I made the turn into the kitchen, I saw the combination of the person I wanted to see the most on the planet with the person I wanted to see the least on the planet.

"See, now that he's here, he can provide a little bit of closure on this situation." Steve's words pierced me like knives, and Mary Ann's crying face provided no comfort.

"What are you doing here? Mary Ann what is he doing here?" My words came out on fire, and I found myself pointing directly at him.

"News travels fast Ted. When I heard Mary Ann was back on the market I couldn't help but come by and find out the truth in person." He walked towards me, and I could smell liquor on his breath. "I heard you got served with papers," he taunted while he poked me on the chest. I quickly brushed his finger off and reached for my back pocket.

"You mean this unsigned piece of paper?" I put it up to his face and he ripped it from my grasp.

"Oh perfect! Okay now how do you sign your name? Is each word legible or does it all kind of blend together after the T?" He put the paper down and motioned a pen towards it, and I grabbed his wrist at the base. With one swift motion his right hand swung backwards and the pen pierced the side of my neck, releasing a mixture of blood and ink onto my shirt. As rage filled my body I reared back and before I could unleash the brunt of my force on him Mary Ann stepped in between us.

"Both of you need to leave, right now, nothing is going to be resolved tonight." Her words were stern and undeterred.

"Hey, we were having a great time until he showed up. Let's get a quick signature from him and we can send him on his way," Steve extended the piece of paper towards Mary Ann and she quickly brushed his hand away. As she finished shooing him off, his opposite hand shot across his body and hit Mary Ann right across her cheek. Before he could reason with his physical power gesture I threw my right fist into his nose, breaking it on impact. Due to his stature, the blow did not make him lose footing, and he threw himself right into my abdomen and we went soaring back into the dining room table. Both of our bodies hit the floor, and we scrambled for position. I punched him in the stomach a couple of times and back in his face again before he rolled me onto my back and straddled me across my stomach. With one swift blow, his right hand delivered an extreme amount of force along the side of my face and I was knocked completely unconscious.

> *The screen remained black in the theater as you could hear a collective gasp at the physical violence projecting on the screen. I looked back at Marilyn and she shot me back a horrified look with her hand over her mouth. I looked up at Mary Ann and my mother as they kept their eyes pinned to the screen, I could see Mary Ann's hands trying to calm her bouncing leg. The screen again showed life, and my eyes fixated in again.*

When my eyes opened the pain on the right side of my jaw resonated all the way down my back into my leg, and it was hard to adjust to the light of the kitchen above me. I regained sense of my surroundings, and saw Mary Ann crying up against the glass patio door with blood strewn across her hands and chest. I lifted myself up and saw Steve laying lifeless on the ground next to me, and a shattered vase speckled all over the kitchen floor. I looked at her and back at him, and made my way over to his body. I put my ear next to his chest and detected the faintest heartbeat, and could hear a soft inhale and exhale about ten seconds apart.

"He was going to kill you Ted," she wailed as she stood over us. Her tears came down and hit my hand, and I lifted it up to her cheek and kissed her on the forehead. I had a ton of things I wanted to say in that moment, but nothing made its way out.

"We have to get him to the hospital!" Panic was beginning to settle in as I put my arms underneath his and lifted the top part of his body up. Mary Ann opened the garage door while I drug him into the back seat of her car, positioning him behind the driver's seat. Mary Ann hopped in the back with him and I put the car in reverse.

My mind was battling the situation at hand and the overall situation with Mary Ann as I continued to look back to check progress.

"He's still breathing, but his blood pressure is dropping. We are running out of time!" She had grabbed a blood pressure cuff and stethoscope as we made our way out of the house, and she continued to monitor his vitals. I exited the highway and made my way onto the backcountry roads I was on just an hour before this moment, and the rain continued to pour down.

"Mary Ann..." I peered into the rearview mirror and met eyes with her, and tears began to come down her face. Silence once again filled the car as the rain pounded the car. The hospital was only about five miles away, and I sped up as the road before me remained empty. The light approaching in the distance sat green, and my eyes remained on the road in front of me. Through the rain, I focused on the light; keeping my speed constant until the light turned yellow. As I approached the light turned red and the car made its way into the intersection.

"Ted!" I looked back at Mary Ann and the world went black.

27

The lights in the theater rose a little as the air in the room stood heavy. Confusion settled in as I couldn't recollect all of the memory that was presented, and deep down the uncertainty of my future started to make me sick to my stomach. The Almighty stood up and motioned for The Hope and The Circle to leave, and a digital timer appeared on the screen. *Fifteen minutes.* The stage soon was empty, and I looked back at Marilyn. She shuffled over to me and shared the chair I was in and put her arms around me. Again, I was finding it hard to propose the proper words in the situation at hand, so I just rested my head on her shoulder and closed my eyes. When our embrace ended, we sat and stared at the clock ticking in front of us, as it made its way down to twelve minutes remaining.

"You'll be fine." Her words warmed my heart, and an involuntary tear rolled down my cheek.

"So, will you." I said as I wiped my tears away, then wiping the tear coming down her cheek as well. As the clock hit ten, a mild panic settled in. *I have to talk to Mary Ann; I have to talk to my mother.* I stood up and made my way to the edge of the stage, and scanned both directions available to me.

I turned around and was met with the teary eyes of Marilyn staring back at me, and I made my way back over to her again.

"What if I never see you again Ted?" She hugged me and remained locked tight up against me. I comforted her and rubbed the back of her head, and found the only four words that made sense in that moment. "You will, I promise." I kissed her on the cheek and propelled myself onto the stage.

The loose spectators in the crowd gasped a little, and I turned around and bowed to them. Applause rained down, and I smiled and blew a kiss to them all. I made my way through the door of The Hope and down a long white hallway. A room approached on the right and I crept up to it. I peeked inside to find one sole body sitting alone, staring at the ground.

"Mary Ann!" The click of the door opening caught her attention, and she made her way to her feet.

"Ted!" She put her arms out and I held her as tight as I could, and glided my hand over her back. "I'm scared Ted," her words were overly sincere, and I mustered up all the optimism I could.

"You'll be fine, we'll be fine, this trial was for the both of us." She nodded at the information as indication she knew, and sat back down with her head buried in her hands.

"I killed him Ted, his vitals were so weak in the car." I put my arm around her. "You loved me so much Ted," her teary eyes stared deep into mine. "My biggest regret in life was not loving you more." As she spoke the lights in the room began to flicker. "You have to go Ted!" She stood up and motioned to the door. As I got up, she hugged me again, as tight as she could. I kissed her passionately, and walked towards the door.

"Goodbye Ted," she whispered, staring at me, and mustered a smile that brightened her face.

"Goodbye Mary Ann." I smiled back; the door clicked behind me.

When I made my way back to the theater, the whole room was empty. There were two minutes left on the timer on the screen, and no one to be found. The door behind me clicked open, and The Almighty and my mother appeared before me. My mother made her way over to me and hugged me tightly.

"Mom, where is everyone? Where is Marilyn?" I spoke frantically, and my mother consoled me.

"Honey, she'll be fine." Her calm demeanor threw me off, but her embrace calmed the panic that was raging.

"Congratulations Ted, I'm proud of you," The Almighty spoke with such a presence it filled the empty room.

"So, you mean…" my words trailed off at my mother smiling through her tear-filled eyes.

"Ted, you have displayed a resilience and determination throughout this whole process, and the final judgment is one that brings an intense amount of happiness to me." He smiled and put his hand on my shoulder, and again I looked at my mother.

"I love you son, I love you so much." She put her hand up against my cheek, and I grabbed her hand. I looked over at the timer on the screen, and it ticked down to the final thirty seconds.

"But, what about Steve?" I looked at them both intently, and they both smiled at me. My mother walked over to me, and spoke softly.

"Ted honey, Mary Ann didn't kill Steve." Her words raised my hopes, and my mind raced. "Steve survived that night, and Ted, you did too."

* * * * * * * * * * *

EPILOGUE

The sheets felt clean and pressed beneath my skin. The light blue hospital gown the donned my body felt thin and allowed air to readily flow up and down my bare skin that rested beneath. The room remained dark and still and was only lit by a couple of machines to my left and the hallway light that was filtering through the thin curtains that were drawn lazily across the window. I raised my hands and looked at them both, front and back, and put them back to my sides. The tube coming from my arm felt tight against my skin, and the clamp on the end of my finger pulsated with every beat of my heart. I reached for the call button hanging on the right side of the bed, and was presented with three buttons, all the same size, and all red in color. The first one I pressed released more pain medication into my system, and through the heaviness that overwhelmed my body I pressed both other buttons before my eyelids became too heavy to keep up.

When I was able to open my eyes again, my morphine induced stupor found a set of green eyes looking back at mine. I extended my hand out to be met by a warm set of hands that held mine steady, and a warm smile manifested itself on her face.

"Ted, it is so nice to see you awake," I gazed deep into the green eyes before me, and I smiled at the sentiments being presented. I squinted towards her nametag, and she laughed a bit at my confused look. "Christina, my name is Christina." I put my hand up for her in recognition, and giggled a little.

"Christina, I am so happy to be here, I really am." She shot a concerned look at me, and I seized a bit before the next words came out of her mouth.

"Do you want to see her?" Her words sobered me, and I nodded back at her, and she guided me out of the room.

I stood at the entrance of her room staying completely silent. Mary Ann was lying lifeless in the bed, and her parents stood over her on the end of the bed embracing each other. When her mom caught a glimpse of me, she made her way over to me and pushed me in a small bout of rage, and then hugged me as tight as she could. I put my arms around her and cried softly into her shoulder, and stared over at Mary Ann. I walked over towards her, and put my hand on her forehead. I looked back at her father who shot me a look of deep concern and sadness.

"She is in a better place." My words offered little weight in the room, even though I wanted them to understand everything. Her father stared at me, and offered me four words of rebuttal.

"How do you know?" I looked at Mary Ann, and I looked at Christina, who just smiled back at me. "I just do."

There were about thirty people gathered around, and I stood in the back, remaining completely silent and completely still. I watched as the coffin descended into the ground, and as it went down the tears on my cheeks followed suit. Although there were multiple people offering their condolences and speaking straight to my face, I couldn't muster words or comprehend them. Little by little people drifted away, until I was alone staring onto a newly filled grave. A steady stream of memories flooded my mind, and although I tried to calm my mind the image of Mary Ann was engraved in my head and my heart. I knelt down, and put my forehead to the ground. I cried hard, and every try at ceasing was faulted, and I soon gave way to the ground. I laid down, and put my arms around the tombstone. I closed my eyes, and the world around me melted away.

When I awoke, there was a red-orange twilight that filled the sky. I regained my footing, and brushed the dirt off the front of my body. I walked over to my car, and got in the driver seat. I drove without a destination, and deep down it felt good to just exist. I was constantly feeling different areas of my body, and running my hands up and down my legs and across my shoulders. The cool air coming from the air vents in the car chilled my skin, and comforted me from the humid heat that still lingered in the air. I pulled into my mother's favorite coffee shop, and sat in the car staring at the entrance. I took a deep breath, and got out of the car.

I stood in front of the counter, and scanned all the available options. After ordering I sat back, and waited for my number to be called. A woman entered the shop, and smiled to me as she walked past. She ordered the same exact thing that I did, and I casually threw out a "good choice" smiling in my direction. Her auburn colored hair danced as she searched through her purse. She shrugged her shoulders, and retreated towards the door.

"Let me get it." She tried to shrug it off, but before she could reach the door I had already covered her drink, and she sat down next to me.

"Well, thank you. Chivalry is not dead I see." She threw her hair behind her ear and smiled back at me, and all of my vitals were once again fully functional. The barista rang a bell behind the counter and I retrieved both drinks and sat back down again. I dug deep to try to find the right words to start the conversation.

"I always find it cute when men are nervous," she smiled, and I returned with a blush that filled my face. "So, Ted, tell me about yourself." She sipped her coffee and gazed at me.

"How do you know my name?" Mild confusion settled in as I took my first sip. She pointed at my cup, and as it sat pressed up against my lips I saw Ted written in permanent marker across the side. I laughed out loud at the situation, and returned the gesture.

"So, what name is on your cup?" she smiled and rotated the cup towards me. My soul filled and my heart raced at the five letters lazily written across the side of the cup.

"Nice to meet you Norma."

The End

ACKNOWLEDGMENTS

From idea to final draft, this book has had more than just one set of fingerprints on it. To Allison, who read along the way and helped me craft the final draft. To my mother Peg, for polishing it to the final product it became. To my wife Lacey and sister Emily, for being the final eye and keeping watch the whole way. This book was fun to write, and I hope it not only is fun to read, but ignites thought in everyone who reads it.